More Praise for Point of Direction

"Rarely do the interior landscapes of heart and mind reverberate with such power against the external world of glacier, water and wind as they do in *Point of Direction*. Rachel Weaver's gripping story of two lovers plumbing the depths of their respective pasts, while struggling to survive in a lighthouse on a remote Alaskan island, wholly satisfies with breathtaking writing and raw emotional truth." —**Gail D. Storey**, author of *I Promise Not to Suffer: A Fool for Love Hikes the Pacific Crest Trail*, winner of the National Outdoor Book Award

"A riveting debut! When Anna and Kyle impulsively sign on to be caretakers of a lighthouse, they tell each other it is for adventure, but they are each running from and for their lives. The lighthouse is starkly situated on a remote island with a reputation for being the demise—physical, mental, or both—of all predecessors. Deeply rooted in sense of place, this powerful and moving literary novel explores how wilderness that enchants us also haunts us, with the very demons we bring to it. *Point of Direction* is a gripping and deeply satisfying story; I could not put it down."
—**Elizabeth Wrenn,** best-selling author of *Second Chance*

"It is rare for an adventure story filled with so much tension and surprise to also inspire deep reflection and wonder, but Rachel Weaver's debut novel, *Point of Direction*, fulfills everything desired from a good story. Anna and Kyle are complex characters with hidden secrets, but the biggest surprise is how much we learn about the people and landscape of Alaska through their story. In Weaver's deft hands, the last frontier holds not just the assumed beauty and danger, but humor, resilience, and redemption."
—**Claudia Manz Savage**, author of *The Last One Eaten: A Maligned Vegetable's History*

POINT OF
DIRECTION

POINT OF DIRECTION

A NOVEL

Rachel Weaver

PUBLISHING

Brooklyn, New York

Printed in the United States of America
10 9 8 7 6 5 4 3 2 1

Ig Publishing
392 Clinton Avenue
Brooklyn, NY 11238
www.igpub.com

Library of Congress Cataloging-in-Publication Data

Weaver, Rachel, 1974-
  Point of direction / Rachel Weaver.
     1 online resource.
   Description based on print version record and CIP data provided by
publisher; resource not viewed.
   ISBN 978-1-935439-93-6 (epub) -- ISBN 978-1-935439-91-2 (pa-
perback)
   1. Young women--Fiction. 2. Lighthouse keepers--Fiction. 3. Man-
woman relationships--Fiction. 4. Alaska--Fiction. 5. Adventure fiction. 6. Psychological fiction. I. Title.
   PS3623.E386
   813'.6--dc23
                                    2014009293

For Mike

1.

WHEN HAZY outside light spills in through the heavy wooden door of the bar, we all turn. No one smiles but me. Kyle's been out fishing for a little over a week, crewing on the *Laura Ann*. I leave the mugs in the soapy water and step into his arms.

"Hi," he says in my ear, his voice filling my body with heat.

"How'd it go?" I pull back to search his face. One of his arms stays draped around my shoulders.

He glances down at me and then away, his dark hair curling wildly, and pulls a crumpled check and a bigger, folded piece of paper out of his breast pocket. He tosses them both on the bar. "Two hundred fifty-nine dollars. That's worse than the last two trips. There's no salmon anywhere this year."

He peels off his thick rubber rain jacket and sits on the nearest bar stool. The wool jacket underneath has a new tear. The skin is pulled tight across his forehead.

I return behind the bar and pour him a strong Jack and Coke.

"No luck out there Kyle?" Charles asks from his usual seat at the end of the bar. He's a regular. One of my few friends in town. His whole life has been lived against this cold gray Alaskan shore.

"No," Kyle answers.

Charles shakes his head, a slow scratching of white whiskers against his wool collar. "Used to be wild in here when I was your age. We'd all get back, pockets full of money, lines of coke on the bar, one drunk after another ringing the bell." He continues shaking his head. "Money to burn back then." He takes a long swallow of gin and turns, head a little loose, toward Kyle. "You wouldn't know anything about it." Charles lets out a slow chuckle. He's been at the bar most of the day.

Kyle gives me a flat look, takes a long drink of his whiskey. I go back to loading beer mugs into a dish rack. I notice again the girl at the pool table, her long black ponytail draped over her shoulder just so, and I want her to leave. The likeness bothers me. I slip my hand into the front pocket of my jeans, where I keep the phone number.

"What about something new, Anna?" Kyle asks, pulling my attention back to him.

"You want something different to drink?" He always drinks Jack and Cokes.

"No. This," Kyle says as he slides the folded piece of paper toward me. "Let's do it."

I unfold the paper, notice the tape on the top from wherever he tore it down. It's a notice from the Coast Guard. They are looking for someone to move out to the Hibler Rock Lighthouse.

I don't know much about the lighthouse. I'd seen it on several occasions that I'd been out in the channel but had never really paid much attention to it. It was two, maybe three hours by skiff from town, in the middle of the narrow channel on a rock not much bigger than the lighthouse itself. I bring to mind the octagonal shape, white with a red roof, dwarfed by the mountains that rise on either side of the channel. I read the rest of the paper. A nine month lease.

"For one dollar?" I ask. "What's the catch?"

Kyle's eyes seem to clear of everything else. I see that he has already made up his mind. "We'd take over the maintenance. It's a win win situation. The Coast Guard doesn't have to spend the time sending guys out there to paint and maintain the light, and we get to stay out there for basically nothing."

Charles has swiveled his stool so that he is facing us. "You've got to be kidding me. Are they looking for someone to live out at the lighthouse again?" He looks at me directly. "Don't do it. Let me tell you what the catch is," he goes on, "you've got to live out in the middle of the channel all winter. You two haven't even spent a winter in town. You just go gallivanting off down south as soon as the wind picks up. It's dangerous out there and I don't just mean the weather."

Kyle turns his attention back to me. "It's nice out there. Peaceful almost. The house is in great condition, the maintenance of the light won't be a big deal, I'll take care of it, and whatever the stipend is, it's got to be a hell of a lot more than that." He swings his arm toward the crumbled check on the bar.

"I haven't heard of anyone living out there," I say.

"No one has," Kyle answers. "Not for the last twenty years."

"You seem to know a lot about the lighthouse." Charles has narrowed his eyes, seems to be taking careful stock of Kyle, who ignores him.

I set a beer down in front of myself and another Jack and Coke in front of Kyle. "The water's a thousand feet deep on either side, you know," I say, leaning toward him, both elbows on the bar.

Kyle's eyes hold mine. I feel the momentum building in him, the first pull of a tidal wave, the first hint of motion already underway. "Come on Anna, say you'll do it."

The beer is cold in my hand, cold down the back of my throat. I hold his gaze, something gathering at the center of me. I think of water on all sides, of myself out there. Nowhere left to run.

2.

WHEN WE met just over a year ago, I was hitchhiking on the ALCAN, the two lane road that points toward Alaska through Canada. Kyle pulled up beside me on the road in a beat up blue truck that had seen better days. He lowered the glass of the window with one hand while he worked the knob with the other. I watched the strength in each finger. I hadn't seen a car or truck in three days. My feet were sore in my boots and the silence of the tundra had become loud.

"You're all alone?" he asked.

My left hand moved toward the bear spray in the outside pocket of my backpack.

"You're heading north?" I asked. Obviously he was, there were only two directions available, and he was driving north.

"What are you doing out here all alone?" He asked with what struck me as true concern. "Get in the truck, some crazy person could pick you up. You have a name?"

"Anna."

"Kyle. Nice to meet you."

I stood in the road and watched him for a few minutes longer before I tossed my pack into the open bed of the truck, stepped on the back tire and climbed in. His door opened, footsteps, and then he was standing next to the bed. Nothing extra about him, then or now, only muscle and bone under a wool shirt and work-pants. "You can ride up front."

"No, thanks." I pulled my hood up, settled deeper into the space between my pack and a stack of tires. Winter wasn't completely over.

Three hours later, we stopped for dinner. After the waitress took our order, I huddled in the bathroom, fingers under the hot water to warm them enough to hold my hamburger.

"How far are you going?" I asked when I returned to the table.

"All the way to Neely. You?"

"Neely."

"You'll like it. Seems like you're the kind of person that would."

"Is that where you live?"

"I fished out of there last year. Fished out of Juneau before that, another couple years out of Sitka. I like Neely the best."

I stared at his olive skin, suntanned somewhere warm over the winter. I watched his hands again and the set of his shoulders. Gripping the table, I pushed back against what was pulling me toward him.

"You going to stay in the back for the rest of the eight hundred miles?"

I shrugged. "For now."

We drove north, cradled between ocean and mountains. As Canada melted into Alaska, the previous two years chipped away from me in small irregular pieces until I was back to that morning on the ice peering into the depths of the crevasse, willing myself over the edge. After years of avoiding it, I was now heading straight toward it. I had written the ten digit phone number on a small square of paper, slid it into the inside pocket in the top of my backpack and started moving north.

As Kyle drove us closer and closer to where it had happened, the guilt started out on its well worn path, clawing its way through me. I closed my eyes as it spread through my body and began to hum. I shifted my weight against my backpack. It didn't help. I took a deep breath and concentrated on the trees whipping past, reminding myself that this is what I need to do, that this is my last choice. That didn't help either. It was worse than usual.

I started to feel like I should get out of the truck. I started to feel like I should turn around, start walking south. I studied the back of Kyle's neck through the window as we sped northward. The smooth arc of skin and muscle, a solidity I had sought on rock walls, a solidity I could not find in myself. I wanted to be in the cab, I wanted to have someone at my side. I knocked on the small window between us. He pulled over and I climbed into the front seat, settling my gaze on the double yellow line stretching into the distance.

A couple hours later, steering wheel loose in one hand, body relaxed against the bench seat, Kyle looked over and asked, "What do you do?"

"I move."

He cut his eyes across the cab, grinning at me again. "That's what you do?"

I nodded. "Utah, Colorado, Yosemite, Arizona, New Mexico."

"Why?"

I shrugged. "Something new each time." I kept my eyes forward, felt his on me.

"Alaska's not like any of those places."

"Exactly," I said and then after some time, "What'd you do before you fished?"

"I tried to go to college, but all I ever wanted to do was come up here. I hated Chicago. I got lucky and found a job on a good boat my first summer and I've been fishing ever since."

"What's that like?"

"Its good. Especially when the weather gets really bad, rain and huge waves—that's really living, you know what I mean? Are you going up to fish? You need to be careful about who you sign on with, I mean I'm sure you could handle it, it's just that some of those guys don't act the way they do in town once you leave the harbor."

"I'm not going up to fish."

Kyle stared at me for a few seconds, looked like he was going to ask more questions, but then didn't.

We camped that night on the side of the road in the sparse trees of the tundra. Not a single car passed. I spread my sleeping bag out and got in. Kyle spread his out ten feet away. A little close, considering all the space around us.

"Why do you move so much?" he asked once he had settled in his bag.

"How many places have you lived in the past three years?"

"Well. . . Juneau, Sitka, Neely and Mexico."

"See?" I asked from deep in my bag.

He rustled in his bag until he was up on one elbow. "But that was so I could fish on different boats."

"Right. Something new each time."

"Why don't you just answer the question?"

"I did. There was nothing keeping me in any of those places. I rock climb. I climbed everything there was to climb and moved on." *And there was always something pulling me back here*, I thought, but did not say.

"There's no climbing in southeast Alaska, unless you head up on the glaciers. Gonna try your hand at ice climbing next?"

"No."

"Why not?"

"Why do you ask so many questions?"

"If you'd quit being so mysterious, I wouldn't have to."

"Go to sleep," I said.

"It's not even dark."

"I thought you'd spent lots of summers in Alaska, you should be used to it."

"It's always strange at first."

He left me alone after that and eventually, fell asleep. I watched the sky, and listened to him breathe for a while before I climbed out of my bag and picked my way through the tundra, wondering how far away was far enough. In a relatively flat spot, I spread out my bag and climbed back in.

I started with as many verbs as I could remember in Spanish and then moved on to kitchen utensils. *Tenedor, cuchara, cuchillo.* Every night I worked to hold off sleep, that slippery place from which I woke fighting, most nights. A roommate came home once with Spanish tapes. What I thought would be something to fill in rainy days that couldn't be spent climbing, turned into an obsession, a tool to use to pick away at the night.

I glanced across the distance between Kyle and me, trying to decide if I should move further away. I'd never woken up screaming, but didn't trust that I wouldn't. There was enough space between us that he wouldn't notice the kicking to get free, unless he was up first. *Plato, taza, sustantivo.* The night darkened around me, my eyes ached from holding them open.

The nightmare had grown. Every night for the past two years, more details added, some subtracted, only to return weeks later. It was always cold and dark and tight. There was always the falling, the blood. Some nights the ice moved while I was in it, pressed against my skin so cold it burned. Other nights, I heard my voice, thin and full of fear, yelling her name over and over, the ice throwing it back at me, unanswered. Other nights, I was no longer sure which way was up or down. Whichever way I chose to move, it was darker than where I had been. Most nights, I heard the helicopter beating against air above the ice while I was in it, heard it leave as I froze, alone, one layer at a time.

The Spanish vocabulary words didn't work that night on the tundra. Just as they didn't work every night. I feel asleep despite the fight not to.

I woke to the soft light of an early dawn. My arms and legs were tucked snuggly in my bag, a thin layer of frost covered everything. I sat up and could see that Kyle was still sleeping. I sat there stunned. For the first time since that morning on the ice when I lowered myself into the belly of the glacier, I had not fallen in my dream, I had not been pinned into submission, I had not lost.

Kyle rolled over. "Morning," he called over, and stretched. I stared at him until he smiled. I did not feel exhausted as I did every morning, I did not feel as though I'd been through a war.

"Did you sleepwalk?" he went on, "because if you did, it's too bad you didn't end up closer instead of farther away."

I tried to make sense of it. I had never found anything that would give me a break from the nightmares. Kyle must've noticed the look on my face. A look of concern crossed his. "I'm just kidding. Probably shouldn't say stuff like that when it's just you and me in the middle of nowhere. Sorry. What do you have to eat? I've got plenty of oatmeal. You drink coffee?"

I nodded, still confused. He slid out of his bag, stepped into his boots and began rummaging around in the truck.

*   *   *   *

Later that day, when the road wound down the backside of the mountains, then ended abruptly at the edge of the ocean in downtown Neely, I got out of the truck. "Thanks for the ride."

"See you around," he said. "Soon, I hope."

I looked directly at him for the first time that day. I wanted to tell him I had not spent the night in terror, I wanted to ask him how that could be possible, I wanted to ask him if he had something to do with it. Instead, I turned away and he drove off down the street. I glanced up at the glaciers hanging between the peaks high overhead. Who was I to drag someone else down with me?

*   *   *   *

Neely sat at the thumb of a long arm extended from Juneau in a narrow waterway carved by glaciers. A deep ripping that left sheer walls interrupted only by a few valleys. Snow covered mountains towered over town and on either side of the water. Steep streets ended at the sea's edge and cross streets were packed tightly with a few restaurants, a coffee shop, a grocery store, and a hardware store. An old wooden dock reached out into the vast stone colored ocean. Fishing boats of all sizes were tied up; some shiny aluminum, others heavy steel, several wood, thick with paint.

From the road, I watched men in rubber raingear move up and down the dock, indistinguishable except for what they carried—tools, buckets, a sandwich for lunch.

That night, I walked to the edge of town to a state park and camped between hemlocks, each too thick to get my arms around. I grew up without the protection of trees. I studied the way branches wove together on this shoreline, felt I had finally found a place to rest. In the late evening light, I stretched out flat on my back and stared until I could see the exact overlap of needle, branch and sky.

The rain started later, sometime toward morning. A slow drizzle, a thick blanket against the walls of the tent. I nestled deep into my sleeping bag, feeling comfortably held under the branches and rain, thinking *this is right, this is what I should be doing, this is close enough.*

I actually welcomed sleep that night, gave in quickly to the rhythmic sound of the rain against the tent. The dream started with the helicopter, me buried in ice. I heard it leaving and then the roar of silence, the sound of blood rushing deep in my ears. I needed to yell, but couldn't. I needed her to hear me, but couldn't make my voice work. I struggled to free myself, but only slipped down farther into the narrowing throat of the glacier. My hands tore, my fingernails filled with ice as I tried to claw my way out.

I kicked and struggled and thrashed until I pulled the wet tent free of the stakes, until it covered my face and wrapped tight around my body. I woke up panicked, fighting the tent and the sleeping bag, unable to figure out where I was.

In those first few days, I kept my eyes on the ocean. It seemed to breathe. Two long breaths in and two slow breaths out each day;

always pushing or pulling at the shore. The wind blew every afternoon and most mornings across glaciers before funneling into the fjord, bringing with it familiar smells and a new horrifying specificity to my dreams.

A week later, Kyle found me washing beer mugs behind the bar. I'd offered to close the bar every night I'd worked, anything to put off climbing into my sleeping bag. My mind was thick with the fog of very little sleep.

"Jack and Coke, please." He had on a heavy wool jacket under orange rubber raingear. I watched his hand, thick with work, wrap around the glass I set in front of him. I decided then that thirty was a few years ahead of him, as it was for me.

"You sticking around?" He peeled off one of his two jackets.

"'Til I run into somebody driving south." *Maybe tomorrow*, I thought. Coming back had been a bad idea.

He smiled, eyes light. "I'll be driving south in six months."

I methodically moved the glass in my hand to the drying rack, grabbed another two and dropped them into the suds. "You working on one of the boats?"

He nodded. "Heading out tomorrow." He waited until I looked up again. "I'll see you when I get back."

"I don't know." I set two mugs in the drying rack, wiped my hands and moved down the bar, away from him.

Six days later he was back. I poured him a Jack and Coke. The night before I had listened to my own screaming, the sound absorbed, lost in the dark ice, I had watched each finger of my right hand turn black from frostbite and then break off. I had kicked and flailed myself awake somewhere around 3am and had walked the rainy streets of Neely until the rest of town woke up.

"Can I buy you a beer?" he asked.

"No."

"How about dinner?"

"I already ate."

He raised his eyebrows, laid a hand heavily on the bar. "You're going to make me work harder at this than I already am?"

My eyes burned with lack of sleep. I thought about that night on the tundra, wondered again if that one night of actual sleep had something to do with him.

"C'mon," he said, "I know there's a lot of us to choose from up here, but I've got all my teeth and a job."

I laughed.

"And I'm really glad you got in my truck, even if you did ride in the back the whole first day."

I studied his face and that same feeling I'd woken with that morning on the tundra flooded me, pushing out the exhaustion. I decided it was him. "Probably not too much harm in you buying me a beer." I pulled one from the cooler.

"Not when you're at work. Sometime when we can hang out."

I watched him stand, noticed again the way his body had been shaped by work, the length of his forearms outlined in muscle from pulling nets.

"When do you get off tonight?" he asked.

"Ten."

"I'll come back."

I watched the door close behind him, cracked open the beer and thought of all the reasons I should not meet him at ten, and then did anyway.

*　　*　　*　　*

Kyle fished all summer, four and six day trips, with a couple days in town in between. I found a small apartment with slanted walls in the attic of an old cannery, and moved in for the season. Kyle stayed with me on his days off and left me his truck to use when he was out fishing.

I'd kept to myself over the past two years. If I went to bed with a man, I made sure I left before I fell asleep. I steered clear of anything resembling a relationship, not willing to attach myself to anything at all.

Kyle somehow absorbed the dream from me or perhaps he was like a thick blanket that it couldn't get through. Every night that he wrapped his body to mine, I slept uninterrupted. I began to think of him as some sort of miracle, a sign that I was where I should be, that I might possibly be forgiven.

It was like adding flour to cake batter, my life into his. A certain dissolving, thickening, inseparability. I would hear him, after so many days away, climbing the stairs to the attic. A certain step, a certain weight that made me stop what I was doing. My body pulling toward his, surprising me with the specificity of need. Always, two knocks and then he was pulling me toward him, that look that was for me alone. He smelled of time spent outside, the salt of the waves carried by the wind, buried in his neck. My hands would begin to move independent of my mind. Words were in the way. I was unable to make measured decisions, only blind leaps.

"Most people don't like to picnic in the rain," he said one afternoon at the height of summer, his hand moving slowly across my back as I made sandwiches in the misty rain at the hip of a slow moving river. We'd been together for a couple months at that point.

"Have you seen these trees?"

He shook his head, moving closer. "I love that nothing about you is normal."

I smiled into his shoulder as he moved close. "I just like trees better than walls."

"I can't believe I found you on the side of the road. What woman hitchhikes to Alaska alone?"

"Here's your sandwich."

He took a bite of turkey and cheese. "You never have explained why an avid climber would come to southeast Alaska where all the rock is covered in moss. Why do you make me ask for any and all information about you? Being mysterious is sexy, but it might get old sooner or later."

I kissed his neck and ran my hands up under his shirt. He set his sandwich down on the rocks. "It's raining," I said. "Your bread's going to get soggy."

"I don't care," he said and reached for me.

When September came to a close and the sideways rain began to pound the shoreline, Kyle said, "Come to Mexico with me this winter." We were in town at the diner. Pancakes, eggs, toast, bacon and coffee spread between us. I had been in Neely five months. I had picked up the pay phone on Main Street once, dialed the phone number, and hung up before the first ring finished. If I kept my head down, never looked up, I didn't have to notice the ice above me.

"Okay."

He tilted his head back and laughed, reached for my hand. "It's that easy?"

"Apparently."

We left Neely on the last day of September, as the wind blew the rain hard against the side of the truck. I settled in next to him on the bench seat as we started up and over the mountains. I liked the way the small cab perfectly contained us from the rain that beat against the trees and the road.

"Tell me more about the town," I said. Despite my Spanish skills, I had never been anywhere I could use them.

"It's right on the beach. We'll drink cheap beer and surf every day."

"Sounds glorious."

"Every fall I think about checking out somewhere else, but when fishing's done and it's time to drive south, that's always where I want to go."

"I can't wait to put my raingear in a box."

"It'll be sunny and warm all winter. We'll pick up odd jobs—a friend of mine owns a restaurant and another guy I know runs a construction crew, but mostly we can just chill out."

I put my hand over his where it rested against my thigh. The idea of spending every day with him for months on end sounded better than anything else I could think of.

The hours of driving stretched into days. The truck had only a tape deck so we took turns buying tapes at gas stations. I stuck to old country legends and he went for eighties' classic rock.

At night we slept in the back of the truck in state parks, in rest stops, or campgrounds. I made us coffee in the mornings in a plastic French press while he stirred oatmeal over the camp stove.

As we passed through the southwest, Kyle asked if we should stop somewhere to climb. "This is where it all happens, right? I saw a sign for Joshua Tree. You could teach me."

"I don't climb anymore. I quit."

"You quit because you moved to Neely where there is no climbing. C'mon, I want to learn, I want to see you in your element."

"I said I quit. I gave away all my equipment."

"Why?"

I took a deep breath, watched the lines of the road. "It was a diversion. It wasn't leading me anywhere."

"Oh. And working in a bar in Alaska is leading you somewhere?"

I looked across the cab at him. He would never understand. I'd given up everything else in the hopes that it would help. I'd run out of ideas. Climbing was the last thing to go.

"What?" He said. "It just doesn't make sense. All you do is climb, work a little, live out of your van, whatever it takes to spend as much time as possible on the rock and then you quit for no good reason? Don't you miss it?"

I flexed my hand the way I used to before I reached up for the first hold, but that had lead me to ice, to nightmares, to being on the move.

"No."

He shook his head, smiled. "You're like a one page story. More details would make for a better read."

I was driving when we crossed the border into Mexico, after six days on the road.

"ID please," the man in uniform said. He lowered his head to see into the cab better. "And your husband's."

I smiled at him, liking the way it rolled off his tongue, one word connecting me to Kyle indefinitely.

"We're not married." Kyle leaned across me to catch his eye, severing that connection quickly before it was fully formed in anyone's mind.

After the border, hours of silence settled between us. I watched the dusty landscape through the window and tried to figure out why he had answered that question so definitively and why I cared so much. A shiver ran through me at the idea of him walking away one day. I glanced over at Kyle. Somehow he had stepped in between the nightmares and me without even knowing it. If he walked away, I would be left with them.

After a full day of confusing side roads, Kyle announced, "Here we are." I climbed down from the truck into the small downtown. The heat rushed at me, a big cushion making everything comfortable. The sea spread out just beyond the buildings, a friendlier version of itself. He reached for my hand.

We rented a one room hut on the beach for twenty-five dollars a week. It had a bed, a hot plate, a table, one bare light bulb and a thatched roof. The bathroom was a separate building down the beach, shared with several other huts. I cleaned rooms at one of the nearby hotels and Kyle worked construction, but never full time. We didn't make friends, although we could have. The rest of the world began to happen farther and farther away as our world narrowed to each other.

We browned in the sun, the edges between us blurring. It

had been a solid month in which I'd thought only of the future and not once of the past, but it was still there, looming. It seemed heading north had only sent me farther south.

We sat on the beach in front of our hut every night after dinner and watched the polite water barely disturb the smooth sand of the shore. The warm air rested against my skin like a favorite sweatshirt. On a night a few months after we'd arrived, I dug my feet into the sand looking for the cool layers underneath while Kyle sat next to me.

"Why doesn't everyone live like this?" he asked.

"Because they like money in their bank accounts."

"I'm serious."

"So am I."

"Why do some people work their ass off just to pay off some lame house?" he asked.

"Some people like to invest in their future."

"Why is everyone so convinced they have a future? Why not enjoy everything now?"

I looked over at him in the bright moonlight. "Some people like to build on what they have, create something—you know, a life."

"Oh come on. That's all an illusion. You build a life, then one day it gets pulled out from underneath you. Why bother building it in the first place?" He rolled on top of me, pressing my body into the soft sand. With his mouth inches from mine, he assumed the voice of an interrogator. "Have you ever bought a couch or had curtains that matched one?"

"No."

"Have you ever said no to some crazy plan?"

"Not in awhile."

He rolled off me onto his back in the sand, spread his arms wide and closed his eyes. "I have found the perfect woman."

I laid my head on his stomach and stared at the sky. I thought of everything he did not know and swore I'd never tell him.

Another night on the beach, I asked about his parents. "You never talk about them." I studied his face. I knew he was an only child, that he had grown up with his mother, but no other details.

"There's nothing to say." He looked away, something closing between us.

"Do you ever talk to either of them on the phone?" I persisted.

"My dad took off, I don't know where he is." Kyle glanced in my direction. "Same old story. Half the population has a dead beat dad. My mom hates Alaska, she doesn't understand why I want to be there. Every time I talk to her she guilt trips me about coming home, so I don't call. Why are you asking me this? It's not like you go on and on about your family. Or anything else."

I thought about what I might say, remembering the sound of my mother's heels in the entryway of our house. Always a fast, definitive clip. The way she whipped her long coat onto the hanger in the closet when she got home from work. Every day she headed straight for the dish rack and the wine glass that never made it to the cabinet. She filled it full, always pouring a few swallows worth into a juice glass for me. She didn't like to drink alone. This was always Our Time. The rest of the time was Her Time. She clinked her glass to mine. I swallowed dutifully, wincing as always, as she refilled both our glasses.

My older sister always made sure she was in her room when Mom got home. She employed the same tactic Mom used with us at all times except during Our Time. That sliver between the first glass and the second when she was happy, before Dad got home and the bickering started, before the bottle was empty and she was loose with too much wine.

I tried to be gone, I tried to avoid it, but the sound of her heels, the way she stirred the still air of the house, slow and comfortably at first, pulled me toward her. I endured the information handed over in Our Time in exchange for the way she looked me in the eye, for that half smile directed at me alone. It was during Our

Time that I learned that my father preferred oral sex to the real thing, that my mother had wanted to be a dancer, had auditioned and been accepted, had kept her pregnancy, me, a secret until she no longer could.

I looked over at Kyle in the hazy evening light. "All I learned from my parents is that it's easier to be alone."

"And that's why you move."

I shrugged, remembering the scratch of crampons on ice, the slide of the heel and the eventual grip of the toe.

"Maybe both our parents had it all wrong," I said. "Maybe there's another way."

As the days in Mexico began to get longer and hotter, we set out north again to make it back for the start of the next fishing season. The cab of the truck pressed in, felt smaller than when we had driven down.

"Do you think we're close?" I asked somewhere in British Columbia.

"No," Kyle said, eyes on the road. "We're still three days from Neely."

"I mean you and I—do you think we really know each other?" I tried to imagine the words, how I would start to tell him.

He kept his eyes on the road. "We just spent six months living in a little hut. Of course we know each other. Or at least we do until you move."

I studied the side of his face. "I'm not going anywhere."

"How am I supposed to trust that?"

"Because I said I'm not going anywhere."

"Hmmm," he said, still looking straight ahead. "But that's what you do."

"That's what I *did*."

Later that day, we stopped for gas and I snuck around the side of the building to the pay phone. The piece of paper was rumpled from so much time in my pocket, but the numbers were still clear. I dropped in a handful of change, held my breath and dialed.

Maybe now was when I'd be able to do it. I waited for the click that meant the call had gone through, waited for the first ring, tried to imagine the bright kitchen into which it was ringing.

The fear that shot through my body was sharp and hot. By the end of the first ring, the fear had dropped into my stomach, so that I had to bend forward to accommodate it. I slid down the side of the phone booth so that I was sitting on my heels, one arm across my stomach. The phone rang a second time. Before it finished, I hung up, ran from the phone booth as if there had been bees, kept running to the side of the building where I stopped to catch my breath before I walked back to the truck.

We arrived back in Neely six weeks ago in early May on a day when the clouds hung three hundred feet above the water, swallowing all the mountains. I could not see the glaciers hanging overhead, but I could feel their presence.

"Isn't it beautiful?" Kyle squinted into the rain, everything around us some shade of gray or black. It was beautiful in a way that demanded something. A landscape that has the power to ask anyone, at any time, to measure all the hidden parts of themselves.

3.

THE SMALL Coast Guard office in Neely is made of concrete painted beige, and linoleum some long ago shade of green. We wait on metal chairs. I shift in my seat and watch the three boys, barely twenty, who all look the same, with their crew cuts and muscled chests. A phone rings. One of them answers it, speaks in a low voice. He stands and says, "Follow me."

We step in behind him, down a short hallway of more beige concrete and green linoleum. He leads us into a small office where a man is signing papers. "So," the man says, before he looks up, "You're interested in Hibler Rock?"

"Yes sir," Kyle says, holding out his hand. "Kyle McAllin."

"Lieutenant Apdale." He shakes Kyle's hand and then reaches for mine.

"Anna Richard."

"Have a seat." He motions to two folding chairs across from his desk. "Are you familiar with Hibler Rock?"

"I've taken a skiff over there a couple times," Kyle says.

The Lieutenant raises his eyebrows. "You do know there's no trespassing on government property?"

"I didn't take anything, I just looked around."

The Lieutenant ignores the comment. I glance at Kyle. He'd never mentioned being on the island before. The Lieutenant focuses on me. "So you're familiar with the remote aspect of the island?"

"Yes," I say, hardening in response to his tone of voice.

"Are you two prepared to keep the building in the condition it's currently in? It's a historic landmark, in addition to being a working lighthouse."

"I'm a carpenter," Kyle says.

The man nods, stares at us. I want to reach for Kyle's hand but don't.

"I see. Do you have a boat?"

"A sixteen foot skiff."

He nods again. "You can pull that out in the winter when the weather closes in. There's no anchorage for anything that can't go dry. It's too deep." That familiar first turn of fear happens in my chest, the feeling I get when peering up at a climb that I know is too hard. Sun in my eyes, gear clanging at my waist, and a certainty that I will fall a good distance before the rope catches me.

"You'll be able to get around the channel in that skiff until sometime in September," he continues. "After that, the cutter out of Juneau will make monthly food and supply drops for you on their patrols. And," he pauses, looking from Kyle to me, "most importantly, you'll be responsible for the light."

I shift in my seat. Kyle nods across the narrow desk. It makes me nervous, to be the source of so much heat and light.

"What happened to the last guy that lived out there?" Kyle asks. He starts to tap his foot, and then stops. "Probably went crazy, huh?" He swallows, hard.

The Lieutenant shrugs. "That was before my time. The late 70s, I think. Heard he just disappeared. No one's lived out there since. We offer leases every so often, but no one has taken us up on it. Until you two." His eyes are full of his belief that we will come running back to town.

He goes on to explain that both the light and the foghorn run on electricity from an underwater line that was run out there years ago. The foghorn is turned on from the Coast Guard station in town based on the weather predictions, but he'd rather have someone out at the lighthouse to let them know if it should be on when it's not and to anticipate problems with either system.

He leans back in his chair, makes a tent out of his fingers as he looks at us across the desk. "Why don't you two take some time to think about it."

Kyle looks at me. I think about moving on, and am certain I do not want to. I think about living out there, where I'll be able to see the glacier of my nightmare, but will be separated from it. A slow quiet place where I could, with Kyle by my side, finally face it.

I turn to the Lieutenant. "We don't need any time."

The Lieutenant shrugs, thumbs through a lower desk drawer, pulls out a piece of paper, fills in a few lines, saying, "A nine month lease puts you two out there until…March 15." He signs the bottom of the paper, then slides it across the desk with the pen, to us.

Kyle signs with a little more flare than usual, a heavy straight line emerging from the last letter of his name. I sign my name next to his, matching the size of the letters. I imagine the two of us all the way out there, matching the force of the wind, the depth of the water.

The Lieutenant glances at the paper and slides it to one corner of his desk. "Okay. A couple other things: We paint the building every year to keep the wood of the second story water tight, the first story is concrete. That will become your responsibility. No need to scrape, just add another layer like you would a boat. You'll find scaffolding in the shed. You can turn on the light and the foghorn manually if the weather zips up and we haven't turned one or the other on yet from here. You'll see the breaker to the left of the front door. Keep up the logbook: boats passing, weather, anything unusual. It might come in handy for us at some point. And don't go out after anyone in trouble. That's our job. There's a small stipend, paid monthly, to each of you. Do you have any questions?"

"No," Kyle says and I shake my head.

"When can we expect you out at the lighthouse?"

"Right away," Kyle says.

"Alright, I'll have the cutter stop by on their next patrol. They check in on you and go over a few things." He looks from me to Kyle. "I'll need the dollar, of course."

Kyle takes a dollar bill out of his worn and beaten wallet and slides it across the desk.

4.

BACK IN the truck, Kyle's right hand drops into place just above my knee and slides underneath. I breathe into the comfortable pressure of his fingers on the back of my leg, the feeling of things held in place.

I study the side of Kyle's face while he drives. When he turns to me, he has been somewhere else. I see the smile rising through the layers before it reaches the surface. "This is crazy," he says, fingers wrapping tighter around my leg.

"Our very own lighthouse." I shake my head and he laughs.

For the first time in days, it's not raining. "Let's go out to the river," I say.

He turns left on an old logging road a few miles outside of town. As we walk down the path, used more often by bears than humans, the canopy closes in above us, changing the light from gray to greenish-gray.

Once we reach the river, I stretch out on the bank and stare up at the sky between the trees on either side of the slow moving water. A gray so thick I imagine one of these river rocks would bounce off it, if I could throw that far.

I can feel Kyle's mind moving fast as he paces at the river's edge before he sits down next to me.

"Are you good with heading out tomorrow?" he asks.

"What's the rush?"

"I'm just ready. Seems like the next step, and I'm ready for it."

"The next step to what?" I push up onto my elbows.

Kyle shakes off my question, smiles, "Come on Anna, you know it's going to be one of the coolest things we ever do."

"I'll talk to Nancy tonight at work. Susie's been wanting more hours anyway. Good thing the attic is month to month."

"I'll head to the hardware store first thing in the morning. Do you want to cover the grocery shopping? Did he mention a generator? We'll need to bring gas."

"There's got to be one." I listen to the slow pull of water, let this new definition of us wash over me.

Kyle asks something else I do not hear. When I look over, he's watching me. "You'll be okay out there, right?" he asks, slowing down for the first time since we got to the river.

"I'll be fine. It'll be you who goes crazy first."

"No one's going crazy. It's a grand adventure, it's not jail."

Sometimes one turns into the other, I want to say, but don't. Instead, I roll toward him. His hand moves around my waist to my lower back. His breath inches down my neck while his hand moves slowly. My skin melts toward his. It has always been this way. Heat and ice. Something outside of reason. His touch, creating in my body a demand for more oxygen.

*   *   *   *

The following afternoon, our skiff is low in the water. A solid flooring of canned goods, tools, and backpacks - everything we own and everything we could think of that we might need. We stand on the dock, peer out together at the horizon, in the direction of our new home. I have on a winter hat in the cool summer rain.

"Ready?" Kyle asks.

For some reason, how I feel does not match the excitement in his voice. "Guess so."

The water stretches out before us, a stone colored sheet pulled tight at the corners. In this kind of weather, the channel is easily passable by skiff.

I zip up my jacket. It's not the cold, it's the way the sky opens. I turn, look over the mound of our belongings to Kyle at the tiller.

He grins, large and unhindered as Neely slips away. I smile back and he lets go of the tiller, climbs over the mountain between us and leans in for a kiss. We both laugh as we are pitched sideways against the caprail with the sudden sloshing of the boat.

As he gets us back on course, I tuck my hands in my pockets, turn my back to the wind. The vibration of the motor keeps my thoughts from organizing. The temperature of the water moves up through the aluminum boat, through the soles of my rubber boots and wraps around the bones of my feet. Water all around, fifty degrees lower than the temperature of my heart.

*   *   *   *

I've never been up close to Hibler Rock, only seen it from the ferry a couple times. The lighthouse is large and white, a two story octagon with a red roof. In the center of the roof rises a second smaller octagon made of glass that houses the light. The island floats in the shape of a tadpole on the surface of the water. A round body on which the house sits, a long tail made of rocks piled haphazardly on top of each other. I notice there are two spruce trees of equal height.

When we get close, Kyle slows down to a crawl. We approach cautiously as the lighthouse looms, huge above us. Eventually, I point to the twenty foot wide beach. "There it is," I say. Kyle doesn't move. I'm not sure he's heard me. I've found the only safe place to land. "There it is," I say again.

He snaps back, nods and turns the skiff, his eyes following mine. I hop over onto the small shelf of rock that is the beach and hold the bow while he raises the motor.

Our bodies collide as we pull together, nudging the boat up onto the beach. I kick a line free from the small gray rocks. "Found the haulout." It's a long line, anchored to two big rocks on the beach, fifteen yards apart which then runs out to a small buoy floating in the water.

"Doesn't look too gunked up," he says.

"No, not bad." I start walking up the beach, running my hand along the line, freeing it of seaweed so it will run smoothly through the pulleys. Kyle does the same thing on the other side of the loop. He ties the skiff to the haulout, then we both pull the line, our bodies moving in unison until we've pulled the skiff out to the buoy so that it will not go dry as the tide goes out. He ties a knot in the line to keep it in place.

"C'mon," he says, walking backwards up the path, reaching for my hand. He's suddenly in a hurry.

I turn and study the skiff, make sure it's not moving out into the channel with the tide before grabbing his offered hand. The rain is light on my shoulders as he pulls me into himself.

We climb the small rise to the house. Mountains on either side begin jagged and white, turn to a green that is almost black, then dive sharply into the sea. In the other two directions, the channel snakes long and thin as far as I can see.

"It's unbelievable." I turn in a circle, trying to take it all in at once, a new feeling taking root inside me, stopping me in my tracks. This is a place where all the rules are different, a place outside normal life and society, a place where I have not yet failed.

Kyle is already at the front door. It is thick and wooden, rounded on the top and wider than most doors. There is no lock. He turns the handle and pushes. Nothing happens. He pushes harder and eventually uses his shoulder to unstick the door.

He falls into a cavernous room built of concrete. A foundation to withstand hurricane force winds. I cough as the damp, mildew-tinged air enters my lungs. There's a window sunk deep into each of the eight walls, one bare bulb hanging from the ceiling. To the left of the doorway, a kitchen hugs two full walls. Wide wooden stairs lead up to the second story. Off to the right is a large square woodstove with a braided rug and an antique rocking chair in front of it.

"Look at all this space," I say. The downstairs alone is three times the size of the attic.

"It's like we're millionaires." Kyle grins.

In the center of the room stands a stark wooden table with four chairs. There is a specific stillness in the house. A thickness that makes me check that I can get a deep breath. "Everything looks so…museum-like." I step toward the middle of the room.

Kyle's eyes jump from one part of the room to another, almost as if he doesn't know where to start. Eventually, he crosses the room to pull back an off-white heavy curtain that sections off the area underneath the stairs. He begins examining the shelf contents, moving things around to see behind them.

I do not feel comfortable enough to touch anything yet. It feels like a space that wants to be left alone.

I study the kitchen from where I stand. It consists of a deep metal two-basin sink with a drain but no spigot, an old cookstove and no refrigerator. There are two propane lanterns hung on hooks on opposite walls. I make a mental note that we'll need to buy coolers to keep food outside the way people who live off the grid in town do. More often than not, the outside temperature equals the temperature a fridge might produce.

There is lots of counter space made of thick, smooth wood and hand built cupboards. I open one. There are plates, cups, and bowls from another era. *Plato, taza, sustantivo*, I repeat to myself softly. I open a second, lower cupboard. Heavy cast iron pots and pans are stacked neatly.

As I close the cupboard, my fingers run over something rough. I open the cupboard all the way, study the number 29 that has been carved into the inside of the door. It looks like it was done with a pocket knife, but it's not sloppy. It is at the top outer edge of the cupboard where your fingers or thumb would naturally fall when opening it. The numbers are two inches tall. "Twenty-nine what?" I wonder to myself as I close the cabinet. Kyle is still under the stairs.

With my hands in my sweatshirt pockets, I give the cookstove and the woodstove and the table and the rocking chair a quick once over. Kyle has stopped rummaging, is now crouched down, examining a row of paint cans that have Extra White / Summer 1973 written across the top in permanent marker in neat, tight lettering.

"That's probably not good anymore," I say, kidding. He doesn't move. "Kyle? What's wrong?"

After a slow moment, he stands and throws me over his shoulder. "C'mon, millionaire."

I laugh, kick once or twice trying to free myself.

"I'm going to show you the bedroom." His feet creak on the wooden stairs under our combined weight.

The metal frame bed squeaks loudly as he presses his body on top of mine. I pull at his shirt, my need matching the urgency of his. When the skin of his chest touches mine, there is nothing but this, right now, Kyle and me.

Later, we fall asleep, piled in the deep depression at the center of the mattress, a government issue scratchy wool blanket pulled over us. I awake to the sound of the wind against the house. I run my hand lightly across his back as he sleeps against my shoulder.

The bed is the only furniture in the room. There is a large window on each of the eight walls, the same as downstairs. A propane lantern hangs from a nail in one wall. Three square wooden posts break up the bare space of the room.

Kyle stirs, rolls over onto his back. "What's that noise?" he asks.

"The wind."

"Ahh," he says with a heavy exhale, waking up slowly.

I press my cheek against his shoulder. "Did you notice the cookstove downstairs?"

"Not really."

"It's a woodstove." I stifle a laugh.

"What?" He pushes up onto an elbow and catches my eye. "Seriously?"

"Yeah."

"Oh damn," he says, laughing with me. "What have we gotten into?"

"We'll have to spend the whole summer hauling wood if we want to eat."

"Ahhhhhhh," he groans, rolling back onto his back. "Hold me," he says meekly, making me laugh harder.

"C'mon, get up," I say, getting out of bed, finding my clothes on the floor. I walk to the nearest window to see how bad the wind is as I pull my sweater over my head. The smooth channel has become an angry procession of three and four foot waves pressing south.

I scan the stretch of water where the skiff should be. "Kyle!" My mind rejects what I'm seeing. I search the beach for the haulout line, make sure I'm remembering correctly where the skiff should be. The haulout line is there, leading to empty ocean. "The skiff!"

Kyle is suddenly behind me, pulling on boots, rushing downstairs. I slip my boots on and race down the stairs after him. The wind pushes hard against my side as I run the path. Kyle is standing, arms loose at his sides on the beach when I get there.

There's nothing to do. The skiff is still tied to the haulout, but is now sunk and hanging from the buoy, pulling it most of the way under. The bow of the skiff pokes through the surface between waves. It was overloaded, too low in the water to withstand what the wind had become in only a few hours.

One wave after another over the caprail had filled it and sunk it. I review what we now do not have. Food, a way off the island, clothes, a way to cook. I think about the steaks I was going to cook tonight, the bottle of wine to go with it to celebrate, my wallet, my favorite sweater, all of it falling to the floor of the ocean, swept over the ledge of the island by the tide, into the depths of the channel.

I pick up the haulout line, lean the weight of my body away from the water.

"I already tried," Kyle yells over the wind. "It's too heavy."

I dig in my feet and pull with every muscle in my body.

"Anna!"

I spin around. "Help me pull!"

He shakes his head, but picks up the rope behind me and together we try to inch the skiff back toward the beach. It doesn't move. Breathing hard, I drop to my knees on the rocks of the beach. "How could we be so stupid?"

Kyle runs his hand over his face, looks back out toward the buoy. "There's nothing to do now, we'll have to wait for the tide. Even then, I don't know…"

I get to my feet and watch the surface of the water boil. Kyle stands next to me for awhile, the wind ripping up the space around us. He takes a deep breath, then lets it out slow. "Shit," he says, shaking his head and turning back toward the house.

"Kyle!" I yell over the wind. He turns. "We can't just leave it."

"It's high tide. There's nothing we can do until there is less water between us and the skiff." I know he's right. Down the shore, something catches my eye. A can of black beans, washed up and bouncing between two rocks. My stomach rumbles with hunger. I remember the jugs of water that were also in the skiff and suddenly I am thirsty as well. Kyle turns toward the house again. I scoop the can of beans off the beach and follow him.

Inside, he sits in the rocking chair, runs his hands over the well worn curve of the arm rest. I pace. "Now what?" I ask. "That was everything we own."

Kyle takes a deep breath. "We'll wait for low tide. If I can get the engine off, we'll be able to pull the skiff in."

"How are we going to get to the engine?"

"I'll swim out to it."

"Bad idea. You have seven minutes in water that temperature before hypothermia sets in so bad you can't swim back."

"If it's at the right angle, I can get the engine off in seven minutes."

"Bullshit. You're not going in the water."

"You got any better ideas?"

"The engine's ruined anyway."

"Right, but we can save the skiff. It's too heavy to pull in with the outboard on it. There's another engine in the shed. An old shitty Evenrude, but it will work. It's our only choice now."

I stop pacing and turn to face him. "You know the contents of the shed? You've been out here more times than you admitted to the Coast Guard guy haven't you?"

"I've always been interested in this place."

"Why?"

He shrugs, glances toward the window with a look I cannot read. "Do you remember when the high tide was this morning?" He asks. The tide book sunk along with everything else.

"11am, I think."

He checks his watch. "That means another two hours before the low."

I sit down in one of the kitchen table chairs and rub my eyes. "We have one can of black beans for dinner."

"Great," Kyle says. "I like black beans."

"Me too."

He crosses the room, I lean into him as he wraps his arms around me.

"We have to be more careful," I say into his shoulder. "We are allowed fewer mistakes out here."

5.

MY PARENTS folded me into myself. The first time I felt light seep in was in high school when my class went to a rock climbing gym. My friends cackled and laughed, went up five or six feet and begged to come down. I started out the same, but somewhere around ten feet off the ground, a feeling more pure than any I'd had up to that point shot through my whole body. The tangle of shame and loyalty, of trying to stand up for one of my parents without sacrificing the other, was pushed aside as cold, instant fear displaced everything else. I scrambled up the wall higher and it increased. Thrilled, I climbed to the ceiling and looked down, just to feel it pulse.

I climbed as often as I could after that, poured over the pictures of rock climbers in magazines every night. Eventually I became entranced with ice climbing, the colder, more volatile sister of rock climbing. I was drawn to the idea of ice and that lead me to glaciers. I read everything I could find about them, stared at pictures in books, fascinated by how thick they are, the rolling hills of deep blue produced by the compression of snow and time. The way they are able to create caves, canyons and ledges, whole landscapes, and then just as easily, destroy them.

The day I graduated from high school, I drove to Colorado. I rock climbed in the summer and learned to ice climb in the winter. I lived out of an old gray van, worked in restaurants and bars, taught climbing lessons in gyms, called home rarely, if ever. Years passed in which I learned how to breathe easy, no longer caught between two opposing forces. Eventually, I got a job leading backpacking and climbing trips in the mountains of Colorado, Utah and Wyoming.

On my twenty-fifth birthday, on a trip in the Medicine Bow Range, one of the other guides asked me what was on the agenda now that I was halfway through my twenties.

"Alaska," I said without thinking. It was a natural progression from the Rocky Mountain West. Wilder, harsher, steeper. I was drawn by the idea of so much ice in one place—glaciers still actively shaping valleys, creating lakes, keeping everyone but the most determined out.

I saved every dime that fall and winter. When spring had a solid hold on the land, I drove the old gray van north. I was headed to the interior, to the Wrangell-St. Elias mountain range, but never made it.

The van started overheating not long after I crossed the border from British Columbia into the Yukon, before I ever made it to Alaska. I stopped in the next town, which consisted of one building. There was a gas station, a mechanic shop, and a hotel in the building. There were a couple tables in the gas station where you could be served from a limited menu. Beyond the building were some scattered houses and beyond that was nothing but horizon. At first, the mechanic, who owned the building and all of its businesses, was thrilled when my van would not start. It seemed he'd not had anything to do for a long time.

He was somewhere near fifty, with blue coveralls and heavy boots. He had black hair, with lots of white coming in, that wisped out from under his ball cap. I sat on a stool in the garage while he clanged and sweated over the van's engine. I had slipped the can of bear spray from my pack into the pocket of my sweatshirt, just in case. There didn't seem to be anyone else around. I made sure the bulk of my sweatshirt covered the shape of the can. After a while, the mechanic announced the problem was with a blown head gasket.

He wiped his forehead with his arm. "You've got a couple

other problems as well, but we can talk about those later. Has it been running hot?"

"Yeah. I dumped a whole gallon of water in the radiator the last time I stopped. How much will it cost to fix it?"

"Oh…as long as I got it all torn out, might as well replace the timing belt that's about to go also… 'bout $4500. Canadian."

"That's more than the van's worth. Forget it." That was also more than I had in my savings account.

"What do you mean forget it? The only way you're getting out of here is to have me do the work."

"Anybody around here want to sell a car?"

"No."

"Then I'll find a ride north with someone stopping for gas."

"Good luck with that. You can stay in the hotel while you wait for someone to stop for gas, it just so happens all the rooms are available. We'll leave the van up on the rail for when you come to your senses."

"I'll camp." Why spend the money on a hotel room when I have all my camping gear?

"You're kidding."

"Is there someone creepy I should know about? There can't be more than ten people that live here."

"No one will bother you, it's just that I have this perfectly good hotel you can stay in for only $50 a night."

"Thanks, but I'm fine camping."

I spent the next four days loitering, asking each of the five cars that stopped for gas if I could catch a ride. No one had room for me and all my climbing gear. I bought food from the gas station and ordered 'lunch' —no further description—from the menu each day, so that I wasn't completely freeloading. I met everyone in town and decided for myself that no one was creepy, but still kept the bear spray in the front pocket of my sweatshirt the whole time, because it made me feel safer.

The mechanic shook his head every morning when he came

to work and realized I was still there. He deduced quickly that I wasn't going to spend the money I had fixing the van. Eventually he produced a middle aged man with a beer belly who he said ran a glacier backpacking outfitter on the Juneau Ice Field. I was standing next to the gas pump watching the long straight road for any sign of a car. "Not in Juneau, who would want to live there?" the mechanic clarified, "but from the Canadian side, the better side of the ice field."

I picked out another Cool Ranch Dorito from the snack bag I had purchased from the gas station and looked at the guide's old corduroys worn paper thin at the knees, his rope belt and his faded t-shirt.

"And he's trying to date my sister," the mechanic added.

The guide ignored the mechanic, held out his hand to me. "Name's Brad."

"Anna Richard." I wiped Dorito residue onto my pants and then offered my hand.

"Bill says you need a job," Brad said.

"I'm trying to get up to Wrangell-St. Elias. My van broke down. I don't need a job, I just want to get out on the ice."

Brad rolled his eyes. "What is everyone's fascination with Wrangell-St. Elias? The Juneau Ice Field is just as vast and more rugged because we get the weather off the ocean. Everyone always overlooks it, on their way up to Wrangell. Kind of like that guy in high school who all the girls ignored because he weighed ninety pounds, but then he grew up and filled out, and doesn't he look good now."

I dug another chip out of the bag and stared at him. "You're saying the Juneau Ice Field has grown up and filled out?" I glanced down the road again. Surely, someone would have room for me and my gear soon.

"So, can you give her a job?" The mechanic asked. "Get her off my property? Last thing I need is some woman sleeping out by the dumpster all summer. Bad for business." Of the five cars that had stopped in the last four days, none had needed any work and no one had stayed in the hotel. The mechanic had about as much to do as I did.

"You ever set foot on a glacier before?" Brad asked. He didn't seem to have anything to do with his day either.

"No."

He glanced over at the mechanic and then back at me. "You better go on home. We get folks like you all the time up here, been on a few hikes down south, think they are real adventurers. They end up lost on the ice and we end up looking for them."

My chips were gone. I was tired of being stranded. I had no idea how I was going to get myself out of the situation I was in. "You're saying that I'm going to need *you* to come look for *me*? I doubt it."

The mechanic gave Brad an exasperated look. "My sister called you a jackass the other day and I said you weren't. Don't act like one now."

"When did she say that?" Brad turned to face the mechanic.

"I'm leaving," I said, heading toward my tent.

"Hold on," the mechanic said. "Brad here, owns a guiding service about eighty miles away. He takes high school aged kids out on the ice for three week long trips, and he needs another guide for the season. I'm going to guess from all that crap in your van that you could do something like that?"

I spotted a car coming toward the gas station, the first one of the day, and kept my eyes on it.

They were both waiting for me to answer, and so I did. "I've guided high school aged kids for the past five years in the Medicine Bow, the Tetons, the Never Summer Range, the La Salles, the Wasatch, the Sangre de Cristo—"

"Sounds great. I'll pick you up in a few days." Brad said.

"I don't want a job. I want to get up to the Wrangell-St. Elias."

"Let me be honest," Brad said. "You don't have many prospects. From the looks of things, you're going to end up camped here for the better part of the summer."

"She'll take it," the mechanic said.

"I don't need you for another four weeks. But you can catch a ride with me in a few days." Brad smiled. "Sorry I was being an asshole."

I watched the car pass without stopping. It wasn't looking up. What was the difference between one ice field and another when you had nothing to compare them to? It would at least give me something to do, some experience out on the ice while I worked on finding a way up to the Wrangells. The season was short, fall up here might as well be winter. I was wasting days.

"Alright." We shook hands and the mechanic slapped us both on the back.

I asked the two cars that came through in the next few days, but did not find a ride north. When he came back, I packed my gear into Brad's truck, said goodbye to my van and left it for the mechanic to use for parts. As we got on the road, I rested my hand inside my sweatshirt pocket on the bear spray.

"How did it go with the sister?" I asked Brad after awhile.

"She'll come around."

He headed southwest. The tundra held on until it couldn't any longer. It gave way to a steeper, greener landscape that eventually gave way to ice.

I was surprised to find Brad's guiding service was actually legit. He pointed it out as we drove into town. It was in a small skinny building that looked like it might have been a house of ill repute in the previous century. All the buildings of the small town had the same old-timey façade. The town sat on the shores of a blue-green lake that one of the glaciers of the Ice Field spilled into. This was the jump off point for his three week trips. He had four planned for the summer, all of them full. He was making a decent living. Owned a house in town that he had built himself.

When he pulled up in front of it he said, "You can crash on

the couch while you get your gear organized. I expect you'll head out soon?"

"Tomorrow."

"The grocery store's not open today or tomorrow. You'll have to wait until Monday to provision. This isn't down south."

I pushed open the passenger door and walked to the back of the truck to start collecting my gear. He came around the truck from the driver's side. In a nicer tone he said, "We can go to the office tomorrow. I'll give you some aerial photos, you can spend some time out on the ice familiarizing yourself with the route you'll be leading."

The next morning, we walked the wooden sidewalk from his house to his office. The front door was narrow, just like the whole building. Inside, it was organized and clean. Brad pulled maps and aerial photos from a series of wide flat drawers.

"You've spent a lot of time out on the ice?" I asked him as he spread everything out on the old wooden table.

"Twenty years."

"Why don't you lead trips?"

"Tired of kids."

He set his finger down at the toe of the glacier by the lake. "This is the easiest place to get on the ice. There's a trail that goes from town around the lake to right here. You'll see a little spur to your right. Take that and you'll end up on the ice. The lower part of the glacier is dry, free of snow, that's where you'll stay with kids and as long as you're by yourself. Get too far north and snow covers up the crevasses. That far up, you've got to be roped up with someone you trust can pull you out if you fall in. No kids up here." He tapped the northern section of glacier with his finger, "You got it? And you stay out of the snow, too. I've seen plenty of hot shot ice climbers like you come up from down south, way too confident. Glaciers are a whole different world."

The next day I stepped onto the ice under a fully loaded pack. The glacier originated on one huge peak that towered far ahead of me. From there, it flowed between mountains in the way of a wide, deep river. I spent the next three and a half weeks hiking through smooth blue valleys of ice, up and over rolling white hills, around towers of leaning ice, jumping the narrow crevasses and peering over the edge of the deeper ones. I marked each on the aerial photo I carried, so that I would know where these yawning holes were when I had a line of kids following me. The peaks overhead were sharp and snow coveredwhen I could see them, lost in a hazy gray fog most of the time. I loved the all-day sound of crampons against ice. An agreement outside of gravity.

I hiked the route Brad wanted me to lead the high school kids, twice. It was a big loop on the lower, less dramatic part of the glacier. After that, I spent the rest of my time below the snow, but higher up where there was more force on the ice. The crevasses were deeper, the uphills steeper, the mountain peaks rising out of the ice, closer. I had to go back to town a couple times to buy more food, but each time I only stayed one night. I felt more at home out on the ice where there was the right step and the wrong step, the safe way and the dangerous way, the ice and the sky and nothing in between.

I walked back in to town the day before I was to report to work.

"Thought we were going to have to send out Search and Rescue after all," Brad said when I opened the door to the office.

I sat down across from him. "How many kids coming in? The trip still full?"

"I've never known anyone to spend four weeks on the ice by themselves," he said, peering at me from behind his desk.

"I like it out there."

"Ten kids. You'll be working with Jason. He's guided for me before, but it's been a long time. You'll be the lead guide. You hiked the route?"

I nodded. "Twice."

"You can either sleep in the shop here tonight or on my couch again. Whatever you want."

"Cushions sound better than a hard floor."

"You've been sleeping on ice."

"Which is why cushions sound great."

The kids all arrived the next day. There was only one flight a day into the nearest airport, six hours away. Brad picked them up in a fifteen passenger van and drove them back to town. That night, we gathered to pack gear. I moved through the sea of gear on the floor of the office, from one student to the next helping them go through their personal gear to make sure they had what they needed and to talk them out of what they didn't.

"You don't need nail clippers, or this razor," I said to Elizabeth. "Or this watercolor set." She was seventeen, with long dark hair that spilled evenly over her shoulders. She had on tight jeans, a tank top despite the cool temperature, and a push up bra.

"Yes. I do." She jammed all three items deep into her brand new backpack. "I'm a painter." She narrowed her green eyes at me.

"Or this full-sized towel. I have another, smaller one—" I stood to grab a more lightweight towel.

"I'm bringing my own towel." She got to her feet as well so that our faces were inches apart.

"You'll have to carry whatever you bring. No one's going to carry it for you. And from the look of things, your pack is going to be the heaviest one out there."

"I want my own towel," she said slowly, evenly spacing her words.

"Fine." I was sick of her already. I started to move on.

"This stupid trip wasn't my idea," she said. When I half turned, she added, "My parents sent me here as a punishment."

"Expensive punishment." I raised my eyebrows at her pack.

"Take some of it out."

She scowled at me as I crouched at the pack belonging to the next student.

That first day out on the ice, it felt good to be with kids again, leading them into a world I had fallen in love with. We headed west, following the route, which consisted not of trails or cairns but of compass points and degree headings. I led and Jason brought up the rear. I kept the pace slow as the students skidded and slid, getting used to crampons and the weight of full packs. It wasn't long before Elizabeth was walking sure footed past each of them, despite her excessively overstuffed pack. It wasn't long before she was right on my heels.

"This isn't so bad," she said. "I thought it would suck, but it's not that bad at all. I like these things, what are they called again?"

"Crampons."

"Crampons. I like 'em. I feel like I could run."

I looked over at her. She was shoulder to shoulder with me now. "Don't run."

By the end of the day, most of the kids had gotten the hang of it, but some had spent all day worried over every step. The mood as we set up camp was not good. Jason and I offered to make dinner to give everyone time to rest in their tents. Elizabeth set up her tent with her designated tent mate and then came into the cook tent where Jason and I were digging out food and stoves and bowls. The cook tent was a small cloth tepee with no floor, less of a tent, more of a shelter from the wind and rain.

"I didn't even know what a glacier was before I got here." She announced as she piled up two empty drybags and sat down.

"You don't want to lie down for a little while in your tent?" Jason asked. He was my age, also a climber, had shown up in town in a truck that he'd outfitted to live out of in order to work less and climb more. His sandy blonde hair stuck out of his winter hat in a way I found appealing.

"You should rest up for tomorrow," I said to Elizabeth.

"I'm not tired. What's for dinner? I'm starving. Can I have a snack to tide me over?"

I found the cutting board and dug my knife out of my pocket. "You can cut up the cheese."

On the second day out, after the discussion Jason led about no sexual relationships, Elizabeth slept with the boy who was quickly establishing himself as the ring leader of the older boys and then began her long vigil of ruthlessly ignoring him. The kids took sides within hours. In a situation where we all needed to trust and depend on each other, she had upset the balance. When I told her as much, she said, "It takes two to fuck."

"Right," I said. "I told Rob the same thing. But it was you who climbed into his tent and talked his tentmate out."

She narrowed her eyes and stomped off across the ice.

That night at dinner, Elizabeth was the first in line. She stacked two burritos on her small plate and found a place to sit out of the wind on the backside of the cooktent. Stephanie, a small twiggy girl one year younger than Elizabeth was next through the line. She sat down next to Elizabeth. Rob was third. When he came out of the cook tent, he threw Elizabeth a look almost as cold as the ice he was standing on and sat down as far from her as he could. Stephanie scooted over, closer to where he sat. With the exception of two girls who were becoming fast friends, and seemed oblivious to the situation unfolding, I watched the other kids, one by one, come out of the cooktent, notice Elizabeth alone, and then join the others with Rob. I watched Elizabeth harden with each choice made.

Later, she crawled into my tent. "They all hate me." Her face was swollen from crying.

I wished I was out on the ice alone, or maybe with Jason, as I crossed my legs to make room for her in the small space of my tent.

"They all say I had sex with Rob just to mess with him, but they don't know, they don't fucking know. He was just as into it as I was and then he said what he said which I'm not going to tell you because it was really mean. Maybe he was messing with me. But I can't tell any of them that because then I'd have to say what he said. They all hate me just like my Dad said they would." Her voice was thick with crying. She broke off into raw sobs, pulled her legs into her chest and dropped her head into the crook of her elbow.

It seemed the gates had been opened, it seemed she had lost her ability to contain whatever she had been containing. It was hard to tell if she was exaggerating. Only two days into the trip, I already understood that she was unpredictable, a river raging through a canyon, either taking out or wearing down whatever was in its way.

But she looked so alone, a perfect illustration of how I had felt at her age. "I don't think all of them hate you," I said and with that, she reached out, laid her head on my shoulder and cried hard.

I didn't grow up in a family where anyone touched anyone else. Occasionally, during Our Time, my mom would brush stray bangs out of my eyes. Aside from that, we all lived in our own small worlds, not crossing into each other's space. No one ever asked how I was doing, how I felt. As an adult, when I did share, it was hard not to measure how often, how much, how soon.

Elizabeth held onto me tightly, disregarding any sense of measured emotion as she cried her way through the past days, months or years. I reached up slowly and rested my hand against her back.

6.

"LET'S GO check the shed to see if there's anything that might help us with the skiff. Do you think there's a winch out there?" I say. The low tide is still an hour out.

Kyle shrugs. "I don't know. Maybe."

When we step outside, the wind whips my hair into my face. I stop walking to gather it into a high, tight ponytail, feeling grateful for the one rubber band I still have. Kyle waits for me. A wind-shredded tarp catches my eye. "I wonder what's under this?" The tarp is tied down over a shoulder high mound about ten feet long tucked up against the outside wall of the lighthouse.

"I'll bet that's the woodpile," Kyle says. "Looks like we won't have to haul..." He falls silent when I peel back the tarp. The wood is moldy and breaks apart in my hands. "Oh," he says. "Looks like we'll need something better than a tarp."

I stare at the woodpile, thinking of all the work it took to cut this much, haul it, split it and stack it. And then to just leave it.

The shed sits down the small incline from the lighthouse, a rectangular wooden structure.

Inside, I wait for my eyes to adjust to the dim light. We are standing in a square room, thirty feet by thirty feet, packed tightly with anything that could ever possibly be used again: full tarps and pieces of other tarps, jerry jugs, oils, stacks and stacks of plastic containers full of who knows what, and lined up along one wall, scrap lumber, all neatly organized. There's a single bare bulb hanging from the ceiling, a small generator to run power tools, several extension cords and a workbench.

Kyle walks over to the wall. "Plenty of wood to build a structure for the firewood." He turns and surveys the rest of the room. "Not sure where a winch would be."

I start on one side of the shed while he starts on the other. I wedge in between two tall stacks of plastic bins and reach up to pull the top one off. My foot bumps into something tucked up against the wall. In the half light, I make out a small bundle. I pick it up carefully with two hands. Small, hard parts under the towel rearrange themselves as I carry it. I set it down where there's more light and peel back the towel.

"Look at this," I say.

Kyle walks over. He leans in, keeps his hands at his sides.

Intact parts of the skeleton lay on top of a pile of clean bones, each a light shade of brown, some broken and jagged. I pick up the skull. "I think it's a bird. Or was a bird."

"What's it doing in here?" Kyle asks.

I put the skull down and pick up the bones of a leg. "Somebody must've dried these bones out before they wrapped them up for them to be in such good shape now."

I look up at Kyle.

"What kind of person saves the bones of a bird?" he says seemingly to himself as he looks over the rest of the contents of the shed. "I wonder what else is hidden in here."

I carefully fold the towel around the bones and tuck it back into the space where I found it. "Didn't the Coast Guard guy say the guy who lived here before disappeared? Have you heard any stories about him?"

"I don't know," Kyle mutters, still scanning the shed.

"You never heard anything around town? Or in Juneau?"

"Just that he disappeared."

I look down at the bird in the dark corner and wonder if I should get rid of it. But someone took so much care with it, it seems wrong to throw it in the ocean. Kyle goes back to digging through crates and shelves without another word.

We don't find a winch. I find a tattered rope. I cannot imagine how it will be helpful, but I bring it along anyway.

Down on the beach, low tide looks better, but not by much. There is fifty feet of water between us and the skiff instead of seventy-five. The wind has slowed, a cold rain taps lightly on the hood of my rain jacket. The early evening has the same quality of light that noon had, it won't be dark until somewhere around 11pm. We watch the bow of the skiff along with the buoy it's tied to, break the surface of the water every so often.

"It's not that far." Kyle keeps his eyes on the sloshing water.

"You can't make it."

"Anna, we can't be out here with no skiff. And besides that, I can't have the fishing fleet going by seeing our skiff hanging from the buoy like that."

"Let's try to pull it one more time," I say.

We line up on the haulout rope and pull. It feels like we are trying to move a brick wall. My feet slip on the small flat rocks. I fall, feel a sharp rock gash my knee through my pants. Kyle drops the rope behind me. "It's too heavy with the outboard still on," he says.

"Let me think," I say, walking toward a rock up by the path that is big enough to sit down on. Blood from my knee trickles down my shin and soaks into my sock.

I hear the splash and then the rhythmic pound of his bare arms against the surface of the water as he swims fast and hard toward the skiff.

"Kyle!" I scream. His clothes are in a pile under his raingear on the beach, his boots folded over so that rain won't get into them. It takes him two minutes to get out to the skiff. I start to pace, hear the sound of wind against ice, feel the weight of a pack, see the way glaciers open, their dark insides exposed.

"Kyle!" I scream again. He is at the skiff. He takes a big breath and disappears under the water. Three minutes. The bow of the boat shakes violently. He comes back up, dives again. Four minutes, five minutes. I am not breathing. There is the sound of the rain and nothing else.

He surfaces between the skiff and the beach, swimming much slower. Six minutes. I watch his stroke, too many seconds between the slap of each arm.

I pull off my raingear, my boots. He switches to a breast stroke/dog paddle, is no longer lifting his head. I wade in to my waist, mussels cutting my feet. He gets his feet under him and stumbles toward me and the shore. His lips are blue, the skin of his arms, chest and legs, grayish-white. "We have to get inside right now," I say struggling to get my boots back on over soaked socks and pants while Kyle slowly stands up. "You're an idiot," I add.

He bends for his clothes, but can't hold on to the bundle.

I tuck in under his arm, balance his naked body against mine. "I'll come back for the clothes."

Inside, he sits in the rocking chair while I run up the stairs and grab the wool blanket. While Kyle wraps himself, I find a roll of paper towels in the curtained off area beneath the stairs, throw the whole thing in the woodstove and light it. I run out to the shed, feet squishing in wet boots, and grab the shortest pieces of two by fours I can find. They don't fit in the woodstove. I leave the door open with three or four sticking out into the room. Kyle's lips are still blue and he's begun to shiver. He raises his eyebrows at me.

"A concrete room is not going to catch fire," I say in response.

He scoots the rocking chair closer to the woodstove. "Your pants are wet. You n-n-need to warm up," he says, stumbling through the sentence.

I pull one of the kitchen chairs over, take my pants, boots and socks off and hang them over the back, close to the woodstove. Kyle opens his blanket and I wrap my body against his. We sit like that for awhile, our bodies warming each other. His body begins to feel less cold against mine. With my head in the crook of his neck I say, "We can't stay out here if you are going to make bad decisions like that."

"Sometimes you have to take a risk."

"Risk doesn't always work out like this. You and me, still here."

"It's fine. Plenty of guys have gone for short swims around here out of necessity."

Kyle's arms are tight around me. I feel myself at the top of a long fast slide. If I let all the words go, I will pick up so much momentum, all of me hurtling toward Kyle at the bottom, him not ready for the impact. I close my eyes, keep everything in place.

An hour later we are back on the beach, both of us in semi-dry clothes. We can only drag the skiff about a foot at a time with the haulout rope, but we eventually get it up on the beach. It is completely empty of supplies. It looks naked and abandoned with no outboard. I pull the plug so that most of the remaining water rushes out.

"I hope that Evinrude runs," Kyle says.

"Me too." I put the plug back in. We'll have to wait for the tide to float the skiff and then pull it back out to the buoy. "Hungry?" I ask. It must be 9:00, although the sky is still bright.

"Yeah."

I find a can opener and pot in the kitchen cupboards, heat the beans over the woodstove because I don't feel up to trying to figure out the cookstove yet. As I stir the beans with a hand carved spoon that still mostly looks like a stick, I notice how thirsty I am.

Kyle is rummaging around in the space under the stairs again.

I find another pot in the cupboard and tell Kyle I'm going to go check the cistern for water.

"Should be nice and full," he says, "it's done nothing but rain this summer so far."

The cistern is a black plastic tank seven feet wide and ten feet tall, that rainwater is funneled into off the roof of the lighthouse. I stand in front of it and bang on its side. The hollow sound of my fist fills up the channel. I check the spigot. Open. Of course. It would have overflowed if left out here to fill for twenty years.

I stare up the channel toward town, and wonder why the Coast Guard guy didn't tell us they'd left it empty, and what else he forgot to mention. I bend down and close the spigot.

Inside, Kyle is stirring the beans. "It's ready."

"There's no water. I just closed the spigot."

"We'll get to town tomorrow. Buy some."

"We'll only get to town if the Evinrude runs." I flop down in the chair next to the woodstove. "When did the Coast Guard guy say the cutter would be by?"

"He just said their next patrol."

"When is that, do you think?"

Kyle shrugged one shoulder. "They are usually two weeks out of Juneau. I don't know if they stop at Hibler Rock on their way out or their way back. I'll get the Evinrude running."

We eat black beans in silence, each perhaps trying to determine the true weight of our situation.

Í set my fork down. "There's probably a marine radio around somewhere we could use to call the Coast Guard if we need to."

He looks up. "You want to cry uncle in our first twenty-four hours?"

The back of my throat is dry and scratchy. I need a drink. Of something, anything. But that feeling that started when I stepped on to the island is still there, is slowly spreading from cell to cell and I don't want it to stop. "No. We'll see about that Evinrude."

He finishes the last bite of his half can of black beans. "Let's go look around while we wait for the skiff to float."

The outhouse is so disgusting I have to hold my breath. "Needs some ashes." I say.

"How did they put that in?" Kyle asks. "They must've used dynamite."

"That might be the best way to deal with it at this point," I say as I push the door closed again.

We walk down to the last small building on the island. The foghorn sits at the tip of the tadpole tail, as far away from the lighthouse as possible, about two hundred fifty feet. It's encased in a five foot tall square structure, also made of wood, painted white. At the top of the structure are two huge megaphones, one pointed up the channel and one pointed down. I try to imagine the channel full of fog. I try to imagine how it would feel to be here and not be able to see out.

Kyle notices the look on my face. "You've got to see the room with the light. You haven't been up there yet, right?" he says.

I shake my head and follow him back toward the house.

In the center of the bedroom, a simple wooden ladder leads straight up through a small hole in the ceiling into the chamber with the light. I climb the ladder first, with Kyle right behind me. Once I push open the trapdoor and climb through, I'm standing on a wooden platform through which the light rises into a room of glass. The view is three hundred sixty degrees of dark gray water, icy peaks and the glaciers that spill toward the sea between them. There are trees and rivers in the lower valleys, rocky shores and sheer cliffs of rock. It makes me catch my breath.

To my right is a small desk with a marine radio, a propane lantern and a brown, hardback notebook with US COAST GUARD HIBLER ROCK stamped onto the front. I flip on the radio, the number 16 blares on the red readout. I sit in the narrow wooden chair and open to the first page of the logbook. There's only one entry. It reads:

12/7/79 1140 *Amy Marie* going down. Relayed S.O.S. to Coast Guard.

The tight script matches what was on the paint cans. There is nothing else except white space. I close the notebook. In the upper right hand corner of the desk, I notice another small carved number 29. Kyle notices as I run my finger over the smooth numbers. He walks over from where he has been examining the light, and bends to get a closer look.

"Twenty-nine what?" he says soft enough that he could be speaking to himself and not to me.

"I don't know." I answer. "Twenty-nine peaks? Twenty-nine more days left? There was another one carved into the kitchen cabinet."

Kyle throws me an uncertain look. "Maybe he counted up all the things he came out here to hide from."

I swallow hard against the idea that Kyle is suggesting that's what I'm doing as I watch him walk back over to the light.

The nautical chart I consulted before we left town called this light a ten second green. I join Kyle and peer into its depths. The light is focused through a thick piece of glass, a complicated looking series of prisms and lenses, Kyle explains, that concentrate the sweeping beam, sending it out over the water as far as possible.

"Looks like it needs some oil." Kyle squints into the dark crevices of the currently still, moving parts.

"What's this one for?" I step to my left, and pull on the handles of the hugest spotlight I've ever seen. It stands at about my chest level and I'm able to swivel it up and down and to each side. "Blinding people?"

"Probably be helpful if someone was in trouble at night."

I nod my agreement as I wander back to the windows, putting my back to the light, facing north, my hands on the pane of glass that stretches higher than I can reach.

Mountains and water and ice. I can feel myself stretch out, as if all this beauty were a couch where I could finally lie down. Avoiding south, I start to memorize valleys, ridgelines, the edges of ice. I remember the distinct smell of ice, that distinct feeling of freedom, as I raise my eyes to the Juneau Ice Field, study it from what feels like a safe distance. When I turn around Kyle is crouching down, elbows out, face inches from the base of the blind.

"I don't think anything's damaged yet, but it needs oil before tonight."

He heads out to the shed for the oil can and I stay where I am, filled with a peace I had not expected. The trees on the shoreline stand strong and still while the water whips this way and that in response to the building wind. It makes me feel hopeful in a way I cannot define.

Through a window to the west, I see that the skiff is still dry. I climb through the trapdoor and then down the stairs to the first floor.

Behind the curtain under the stairs, there are four shelves all neatly organized, one dedicated to cleaning supplies. Bleach, Lysol, mildew spray, all the labels bubbled, some of the words dripping.

I pick up the mildew spray. There is a stack of rags, all precisely folded. I pick one up, unfold it. A square of someone's t-shirt, faded from black to blue. I study the letters on the square in my hand wondering about the man who chose this before us, why he kept carving the number twenty-nine into the furniture. I unfold several others until I piece together CHICAGO TRIBUNE.

Kyle walks in with the oil can.

"Look," I say pointing at the lined up t-shirt pieces. "The bird guy worked at the *Chicago Tribune.*"

"Or maybe just read it," he says as he heads up the stairs.

As I scrub at the wall with one square of t-shirt soaked in mildew spray, a small section of gray eventually turns white. I look around at the eight gray walls of the room. "Gross."

I have one quarter of one wall back to white when Kyle comes down the stairs. "Ready to give me a hand with that Evinrude?"

In the finally fading light of the day we carry the outboard down to the beach. The skiff floats in a couple feet of water. We climb in and wrestle the motor into place at the stern. Kyle goes back for gas. We push the skiff out into water deep enough to put the motor down. I stand in water just below the top of my boots and watch while Kyle stands in the boat over the Evinrude. He attaches the gas line and primes it. "Not sure how long this gas has been sitting. Probably has a fair amount of water in it." He glances at me. I keep quiet. Water makes engines seize.

He pulls the chord and it breaks. He cusses, snaps the hood off and unwinds the chord, ties it back together and re-winds it. The skiff, still tied off to the haulout, has floated further from me. In the gathering night, Kyle is cloaked in shadows. I watch his hands move over the individual parts of the motor, recognize the true emergency in our situation in the way he stands. He is working against the dark, the wind, the distance from town. He pulls again. Nothing. It is getting dark fast, the wind is picking up. He pulls again and again. After seven or eight pulls, the Evinrude turns over, catches and then dies. We both let out a holler. If it catches once, it'll catch again.

Behind us, the light snaps on. We both turn, the wind hard against our backs, to watch the slow sweep of green across the surface of the water, over the island and back out over the water again. The light gives everything it catches an unreal quality, which is then replaced by a darker dark. A silence falls as the sea, the rocky shore, Kyle and I, wait to be caught again.

7.

THE NEXT morning, we peer out the window together. The ocean stretches out flat and tight.

Kyle rolls out of bed and pulls on yesterday's workpants piled on the floor. "I'll go see about that Evinrude, then we can run to town for water and food and maybe even get a load of wood before the wind picks up this afternoon. We'll have to make sure the chainsaw in the shed works." He breathes out audibly. "I'm ready for town."

I turn over onto my back in time to see him stepping into his boots. He's out the door before either of us can say anything about how much water is in the gas, about how far it is to town, how few boats go by to help out a couple people in a skiff with an outboard that won't run.

I take a deep breath, get myself ready for the day. Even if we do make it to town, even if we do have a skiff that runs, it seems impossible, all the things we have to do: cut, haul, split, and stack twenty or thirty skiff loads of wood, build somewhere to put it, paint, do something with the disgusting outhouse *like burn it* I think, build a greenhouse if we want to eat fresh vegetables more often than once a month, then plant it and figure out how to heat it. All this in the next two months before we pass through the heavy door of fall when the channel will become impassible in our skiff. That's if the Evinrude runs. If not, both our savings combined isn't enough money for a new outboard.

I look out the window again, this time south toward Juneau, count the peaks until I know I'm looking at the right one. I can just make out the ribbons of glaciers wrapped around the peak like a heavy loose shawl. I study the southernmost glacier, that last landscape I knew as intricately as I know the distance between Kyle's shoulder and hip and feel a queasy certainness that this is where I need to be. I close my eyes against it, get dressed quickly.

My thirst has manifested into a thick film coating my mouth and throat, an almost frantic desire. When I step outside, the loud whine of the outboard comes up from the beach. Kyle's got a plastic bin full of tools balanced on one of the benches of the skiff. The day is still, the cloud layer high above the mountains on either side of the channel. He looks up and smiles as I approach.

"You did it," I say over the clatter of the idling outboard.

"We better go right now before this thing craps out."

I climb in, I don't have anything to bring except what I have on. The Evinrude sputters when he drops it into gear, but then evens out into a clunky, hammering sound that gets us moving. As we head up the channel at half the speed of our previous outboard, I watch the lighthouse grow smaller and smaller behind us.

The Evinrude dies twice on the way into town. The pull cord breaks again, and the gas line leaks, but Kyle coaxes it until the harbor comes into view.

I have mixed feelings as we pull up to the dock. Part of me wants to be quick, head back out as soon as possible, the other part wants to hug everyone I see, tell them what we've been through, but mostly, I need water.

I tie up the bow of the skiff while Kyle ties up the stern. We cross the street then go separate ways; Kyle to the diner where I will meet him after I go to the bank. His wallet was in his back pocket when the skiff sank. I go straight to the bathroom, scoop handfuls of water from the faucet, drink until it seems my belly can't hold any more, then rest my head on the sink. I wait in line, feeling much better, explain to the teller that my wallet sank. This is not new news in a town of fishermen. The teller recognizes me and lets me take out cash. At the diner, Kyle has ordered us two large coffees and orange juice and extra breakfast.

At the grocery store, we fill two carts with food and bottled water. We go back to the bank and dip money from both our savings. At the hardware store we buy sleeping bags and a camp stove and flashlights, coolers and a couple dry bags, an emergency kit for the skiff, work pants, wool shirts, a couple sweaters each and a couple duffle bags to stuff everything in. I have to cross the street to the one women's store in town to buy underwear and an extra bra.

Just before noon, we stand on the dock again, our skiff loaded full, as it had been the previous morning. I peer out at the horizon, in the direction of the lighthouse. I think about the view from the room with the light, that feeling of almost peace that rose in me as I stood up there, and I want to be back.

"Can you think of anything else we should pick up?" Kyle asks, standing with his hands in his pockets on the dock.

"I don't think the Evinrude will be able to move the skiff if we add anything else to it. Besides, we've got to get going before the afternoon wind starts."

I climb in first, and Kyle eventually follows. We cough and sputter our way back out to the lighthouse. The two hour trip takes three and a half, the wind piling up on itself more and more with each hour. We unload the skiff right away.

With the counter full of food and drinking water, the coolers full and outside, I begin to make mental lists of everything that needs to be done now, as well as everything that can be done later to make this place habitable, to force ourselves into a reluctant house.

As I count off the most pressing chores to Kyle, he sits down at the kitchen table. His eyes wander from me to the various parts of the room. I walk over to the window, gauge the wind by the height of the waves. "We can't get wood today. We'll have to head out first thing tomorrow morning and every morning after that until we have enough."

"Anna, relax. We have endless days out here, we don't have to do everything this week. We can keep burning scrap two by fours for cooking until we have wood split. I'm gonna go poke around in the shed."

"Who knows how many calm days we're going to have? There might not be another one for a week. We need to take advantage of every break in the wind we get. Do you realize how much wood we're going to need for the entire winter if we are cooking *and* heating with it?"

Kyle raises his eyebrows, looks out the window. He moves slowly, the way he does when he's not slept well, when something is on his mind and he's not able to work through it. "We'll see what tomorrow morning looks like."

That afternoon, Kyle goes through the wood in the shed and pulls out pieces that can be used to build the roofed structure that will stand against the house and cover the wood pile. I spend hours scrubbing the mildew from the rest of the walls. I take a break to examine the cookstove. It is an exact replica of something I saw once in a settler's museum behind a thick rope in a room packed full of dishes and pails and washboards from a dustbowl era kitchen.

There are two doors on the front, one much bigger than the other, and above, a wide flat surface with removable round plates—burners of sorts. I open the two doors and figure out that the bigger one is where the fire is supposed to be built, the other I guess is a warming drawer. I hook the round wire handle through the small hole in one of the round burners and find that I can peek in to check on where the fire would be burning from the top as well.

I head out to the shed to collect some wood scraps for tonight's dinner, which I drop into a five gallon bucket. I also find a hose, connect it to the cistern, and run it inside through a window. That way, once it's full again, we won't have to carry water. I cut a small piece of Styrofoam to fit the open space of the window and wedge it in, duct taping the edges to keep the rain out. I go after the outhouse next with two bottles of Lysol and a can of paint.

By the time it's dark, late that night, the muscles in my arms ache audibly from all the work. I light the two propane lanterns and like the soft glow they produce. As I spread out the fire in the cook stove to lessen the heat for our grilled cheese sandwiches, I tentatively rest against the feeling that we will have heat and a way to cook and enough water that we won't have to ration. I glance at the counter full of water in jugs as the wind pushes hard against the house.

Kyle comes in once it's dark out. "I found some cedar shingles to make a proper roof. We'll have the driest wood around." He glances around the room. "I didn't realize the walls were actually white in here. Looks much better. How's the outhouse?"

"I don't think we'll have to burn it."

"Great news." He sits across from me and I move a grilled cheese sandwich from the pan to a plate for him, relaxing further into the idea that we are running a household together.

After dinner, I climb the stairs to the room with the light. My eyes follow the beam of green light as it travels across the choppy water. The ice high above is a hazy yellow green, the edges of rock are black against the gray-black sky. I sit down at the small wooden table in the corner and slide the logbook in front of me. I read again the S.O.S. entry from 1979 and stare out at the uneven surface of water, trying to imagine someone's shaky voice across the radio calling for help. I reach over and turn it on. The number sixteen blares on the readout in bold red numbers.

I pick up a pen and write in a careful script:

June 17, 2000 Wind out of the north, 25-30 knots, 1000 ft. cloud ceiling, no rain.

I smile, feeling like the keeper of this part of the channel. I watch the wind on the water and eventually reach into the front pocket of my workpants, pull out the crumpled piece of paper that I have carried every day since I began hitchhiking north. I spread it out on the desk, stare at the ten digits of the phone number. There is no phone on the island, I should put the number away I think, but have become attached to it. It feels like maybe I am moving in the right direction if I carry it with me. I wonder what it would've meant if it had sunk along with everything else. I fold it back up, along the creases and put it back in my pocket.

I carry the marine radio down to the kitchen. Kyle recognizes several voices right away, skippers he'd worked for or knew. The others we give names to. The Fat Man we call one of them, the Screamer, another. It rounds out the space to have more voices in the house.

*   *   *   *

The next morning, we wake to a sturdy wind. We cannot take the skiff out in it. Instead, we continue with the chores of the island, while the wind pushes everything south. The following morning is the same.

It is not until the fifth day that we are able to venture out. We cross at the shortest distance. The shore is black and green, without definition. Kyle keeps the throttle wide open, until three quarters of the way across the channel when the Evinrude dies. He pulls the cover off, begins to operate. It coughs twice, dies again. He grabs a wrench out of the toolbox he's brought along from the shed. Without stopping or looking up he asks, "Can you tell which way the tide is pushing us? How much time do I have?"

I watch the shore, watch our relationship to it change. "Toward the mainland. You've got awhile." My eyes move across the floor of the skiff—chainsaw, mix, water, lunch, cataloguing what we've got to determine how long it will last us if we get stranded. The new emergency kit we bought in town is duct taped just under the caprail. I'd insisted on an extra flare for it. "Can you tell what's wrong?" I ask.

"Yeah. Hold these." He hands me three bolts and two washers. He clanks around some more, replaces the bolts, tells me to cross my fingers then pulls the cord and the outboard roars to life. "This thing sucks," he says as he sits back down.

We parallel the beach looking for a clearing behind the thick row of trees. We find one, pull the skiff up and hike the short distance into a muskeg, a wetland green with summer. On the edge of the creeping muskeg are trees recently overcome with the acidity of the soil, the abundance of water. Standing dead, perfect for birds or woodstoves.

The chainsaw breaks into the smooth sounds of the forest, everything else falling into silence because of it. I drop two trees onto the squishy mat of the muskeg. As I cut limbs, Kyle piles them up then drags them into the forest. His body works close to mine, anticipating what I will do with the saw. He knows my next cut, knows when he can be close, when I need more room.

As I cut the limbed trees into rounds, he begins to haul them to the skiff. When I feel the first hint of wind, I throw the break on the saw. Kyle looks up. His eyes follow mine to the tops of the trees which are just starting to sway. I finish bucking the last dropped tree then shut the saw down. The sound lingers in the air until it's diluted by seagulls at the shore.

I wipe the gritty layer of sawdust off my face with my upper arm. My rain jacket, pants and hands are covered as well in fine sawdust that the misty rain has turned into a dirty grime.

We make three more trips to the skiff with wood. I can only carry one of the heavy round sections at a time. When we get back to the island, we will split them into pieces that will fit into both the woodstove and cook stove. Kyle carries two at once. We pack them into the skiff, pushing it out into deeper water as it sits lower and lower with the weight of the wood. I tie a red rag around the branch of a tree on the shore so we'll find this spot again.

"We have enough time to get the rest," Kyle says when he notices what I'm doing.

The lower branches of the trees are now beginning to move in the wind. "I'd rather not risk it. I don't want to get caught out, riding so low in the water."

"It's fine."

"I said no." We stare at each other across a short distance on the rocky beach.

"What's wrong with you?" Kyle asks. "You're acting like you never spent any time in the backcountry. What about all that time guiding and climbing? Were you this stressed out all the time?"

I continue to stare at him. "We sank it once already."

His eyes flash. "This is stupid. It's hardly even windy yet, but we can go if you're that worried." He unties the skiff. "I thought you'd be different out here."

I climb into the skiff. "I'm just trying to act smart."

"You're acting scared." He walks the skiff out farther into the water until he's at the top of his tall rubber boots and climbs in. "It doesn't make sense, I mean you hitchhiked the ALCAN alone."

"That's different."

"Why?"

"Because I wasn't responsible for anyone but myself."

Kyle rests his hand on the outboard tiller as we float, pulled along by the tide. He hasn't started the motor yet. "You feel responsible for me?"

"If I hadn't said yes to this, we wouldn't be out here."

"You're not responsible for me Anna, you're only responsible for yourself."

"We're going to run into that rock." I point to the large rock sticking up out of the water behind him. He looks over his shoulder, mutters some profanity and pulls the cord three times before it sputters to life a few feet from the rock. The loud hammering fills the space between us.

*   *   *   *

That evening, I heat water on the stove and we bathe using pieces of the cut up t-shirt as washcloths. It's a quick business, the cold of the room attaching itself to me as soon as my skin is wet. I designate one of my shirts as a towel, which sort of works. We change into dry clothes as quick as possible and stand next to the woodstove to warm up the rest of the way.

On the sixth day that we are on the island, the Coast Guard shows up as we are unloading wood from the skiff onto the beach. We both stop and watch as the thin white cutter slows to a stop two hundred yards off the coast of the island. They lower a small rubber skiff over the side and two uniformed men climb in.

When they reach the island, I see that they are clean cut and young, the type that order two Budweisers at a time at the bar. Their matching float coats read Juneau Coast Guard in bold letters.

"How's it going?" The one with the freckles says.

"Good." Kyle steps forward to guide the bow around the rocks and up onto the beach.

"So you guys decided to live here?" The thin wiry one asks as they climb out of the skiff.

"Yeah." I meet his gaze.

"Captain sent us over to show you what we do when we stop in for maintenance. It's pretty simple, you've probably figured most of it out by now." The freckled one seems to be in charge. We follow him out to the shed where he points out tools for working on the light and then up to the house. He opens the front door as if he were not intruding. The feeling that this is my house overwhelms me, that he should let one of us open the door, invite him in.

In the room with the light, he points into the depths of the moving parts and Kyle asks a couple questions and I want them gone. I want to be out here alone with Kyle making this house into our home.

I leave them to the light, head back downstairs. I'm relieved when they finally climb back into their skiff, head back out to the cutter. I watch the other men on board pull the skiff up, secure it on deck. The engines slowly build as the cutter gets under way again. I watch them disappear up the channel and feel the space of the island becoming ours again.

For the next two weeks Kyle and I spend each morning on shore dropping trees and hauling wood. Each afternoon, once the wind picks up, we work on the island. We split wood, begin putting together the scaffolding to start painting the house, haul wheelbarrow after wheelbarrow full of moldy wood down to the ocean and dump it, and sketch out plans for a greenhouse.

"It has to be low to the ground." Kyle cuts each of my penciled walls in half, "because of that damn wind."

In the evenings, Kyle methodically goes through the plastic bins in the shed. He is in there for hours at a time, after which he often walks the perimeter of the island. I join him one night on his walk, but he doesn't talk much. Any reply is a short one syllable, so I leave him to his evening walks alone.

I continue to record wind speed, the name of any boat passing by, rain or no rain in the logbook. I learn how to wash clothes by scrubbing the fabric between my knuckles. I string up an old bowline I find in the shed over the woodstove as a drying line.

One afternoon, after greasing pulleys on the haulout down at the beach, I hear Kyle laugh just before I open the door. I realize that I have not heard it in a while.

He says into the radio, "No more standing in the rain for no pay like you sorry suckers." He's in front of the window, his back to me. He turns and points to the *Laura Ann* out in the channel.

I walk to the window and stand next to him, watching the boat slowly pass by. I hook my thumb into one of his belt loops.

"Well, it's not the same without you on board," Jimmy, the deckhand Kyle worked with the previous two seasons, says over the radio.

"I'm sure you're getting by just fine."

"Well, there's not as much cussing at dawn and no more stories about—"

Kyle interrupts his transmission by transmitting over him, "You guys catching anything yet?"

I look up at him, want to know what he's grinning at, but he keeps his eyes on the boat through the window.

Jimmy's voice has the end of a laugh in it. "No. It's all going to turn around this trip, though, I can feel it. Alright Kyle, I'll holler at you next time we come by, especially if it's three in the morning."

"Good luck out there."

"You too. Laura Ann back to 16."

"Hibler Rock back to 16."

That afternoon, I climb the ladder. I circle the light on the wooden platform, water stretching beneath me, mountains rising above, my life and Kyle's fitting between the two. The sun, still hours from setting, is weak behind a thick layer of high clouds. I stand with my back to the light, where the boards of the wooden platform meet, face north and let my eyes rest where the two closest panes of glass touch. I lay my palms lightly on the first pane, continue to memorize the sharp edges of ice, the steep face of rock, the smooth valleys in between, my own reflection a part of each.

8.

THE NEXT morning we get an early start. The water is choppy enough that we decide to split the wood on the beach rather than cut more from the mainland. We take turns; one of us splits while the other hauls wood ready for the woodstove up to the house in the wheelbarrow. I take the first shift with the ax, working until the muscles in my shoulders and arms ring with every strike.

"Trade?" I ask Kyle the next time he returns with the wheelbarrow.

"Sure."

With his first few swings, I see how much I'd slowed down over the course of the morning. I load the wheelbarrow, head up to the house and unload it, and grab some water for both of us and a couple granola bars from inside. As I make my way down the path, I stop to pull my hood up. A slow misty rain has started. When I look up again, Kyle has fallen still. The ax rests against his leg as he watches a skiff approach from the direction of Juneau. It's much larger than ours, built to handle rougher weather, but still a long ways away from either Neely or Juneau on a day that the weather will certainly build.

Down on the beach I hand Kyle a bottle of water and offer one of the granola bars.

"Thanks." He tears open the wrapper and eats half of it in one bite. The skiff comes around the side of the island, not close, but close enough that I can make out the two big outboards at the stern of the aluminum boat and one man at the wheel inside a covered wheelhouse. He suddenly drops into neutral.

"What's he doing?" Kyle asks.

The man doesn't move.

"Looks like he wasn't expecting to see us here," I say.

The skiff is now being pushed by the tide, away from the island. The man is still staring at us. He has not moved, and neither have we.

"Why's he staring at us?" Kyle asks.

The skiff dips sharply into the trough between two waves as it gets sideways to the current, which seems to be enough to startle the man back into action. He drops the outboards into gear, swings around and moves a little farther out into the channel. He busies himself at the stern of the boat with his back to us. He throws a buoy and a long line over.

"Is he setting halibut gear?" Kyle asks. "What the…"

I can't make out any details. The man is any man in southeast Alaska in the uniform of thick rubber raingear and tall rubber boots.

"It's too deep in the channel for halibut," Kyle says.

"He's probably fresh up from down south, doesn't know any better yet," I say.

The man feeds out the line with a baited hook every twenty feet, that is supposed to lie on the bottom where the halibut are.

Kyle shakes his head, eats the rest of his granola bar, tries to put the empty wrapper in his pocket until he remembers he doesn't have any in his raingear. He hands the wrapper to me.

"I don't have any pockets either, fool." I have on the exact same raingear that he does in a smaller size.

He smiles and stuffs the wrapper in the top of his boot.

We work through most of the wood on the beach as the morning lengthens into afternoon. We are inside drying out and warming up when the man comes back in the skiff to pull his halibut gear. I watch him through the window.

"Looks like he didn't catch any halibut," I say. "Not even a rock fish."

Kyle gets up from the rocking chair and joins me at the window. "Of course not. It's too deep out there for his gear to reach the bottom."

We watch the man working quickly, moving efficiently between the side of the boat where he is pulling in the long line and the wheelhouse where he is making small adjustments to keep the boat moving in a straight line so as not to run over his line and tangle it in the prop, hard to do with wind and a changing tide.

Kyle watches him for a few minutes. "Looks like he knows what he's doing otherwise, though."

When all the gear is on board, the man quickly coils the long line at the stern and stows the buoys.

"Was he out there all afternoon?" I ask. "I didn't notice him after he set the gear."

"He took off back toward Juneau while it soaked."

The man makes a wide arc around the island, getting tossed by the building waves. Instead of heading back toward Juneau, he crosses the channel, toward the mouth of the salmon stream.

"Now he's going to fish salmon?" Kyle asks. "That stream is empty until the cohos run in the fall." We watch him beach the skiff, a tiny figure jumping over the side, feeding out a line and setting the anchor so that the skiff will float as the tide comes up.

"If he gets the length of that line wrong, he'll sink his skiff, right? I mean if it's too short, it'll get pulled under right?" I ask.

"Either that or the anchor will pull loose and his skiff will be carried down the channel without him on it. Ballsy move if he doesn't know what he's doing. He'd be better off making a run for Juneau, even this late in the day."

The man pulls a small inflatable dinghy and a couple dry bags off the boat, leaves them on the beach and then disappears into the woods. "Looks like he's decided to camp since the wind's come up. Do you think he's okay?"

Kyle shakes his head and shrugs. "He knows we're here. He

can call us on the radio if he needs something."

I drop my eyes to the marine radio on the table. As I walk past, I make sure it's on.

That night I can't sleep knowing someone is right across the channel. It feels like we're being watched. I want to lock the door but there is no lock. I slip out of bed without waking Kyle and climb the stairs to the room with the light. Peering into the night toward the salmon stream, I can make out nothing until the light swings by. In one quick flash I see that his boat is still there, floating on its anchor. I count ten seconds under my breath, wait for the next flash and study the beach but I can't see a tent or any other sign of him. I wait for the light to make its slow revolution, and again see no sign of him other than his skiff.

I climb down the stairs and lie next to Kyle. I follow the light in its arc around the room, listening to the wind against the house, to Kyle's steady breathing for what seems like hours. I drift off at some point and wake to Kyle sitting up in the pale light of morning peering through the closest window. "That guy is gone," Kyle says.

With the first of July, the everyday rain settles in. A slow steady drizzle that blows like curtains across the channel. At all times, I can hear something dripping.

We continue the work of hauling and splitting wood, I learn to bake bread in the cookstove which is a long slow process of under and overcooked loaves. Kyle and I work together sometimes, but more often I work around the house while he works on the structure that will cover the wood or some other outdoor project. When we take breaks, I head up to the room with the light and he walks the perimeter of the island, hands pushed deep in his pockets, peering out across the water. I watch him from afar, the rain between us.

We decide to focus on the greenhouse while we wait for

a break in the weather to start painting. It takes three trips to Neely across two days to pick up the paint from the Coast Guard office and all the supplies we need for the greenhouse. I also pick up the fluffiest towel I can find and two proper washcloths for bathing.

"Should we stay the night in town?" Kyle asks each time we are there.

"No, let's go home."

In the slow steady rain, I swing the pick ax hard, working to level out the area we have cleared for the greenhouse. Kyle does the same just off to my left. In the time that we have been at the lighthouse, we have developed a second language, one without words. Our bodies move, bent toward the same goal, working from different angles. I wonder if we are exchanging a language of words for one without. I wonder if it is possible to have both or if one begins to replace the other.

That night, after we make love, I lie tucked against his lean body, his arms loosely around me. I listen to the small sounds of the room, to Kyle drifting toward sleep, and wonder what we are doing out here. Avoiding life? Living it?

Eventually, Kyle's breathing changes. He relaxes fully against me. In my mind, I see the lighthouse as I did that first day we drove up in the skiff. It towers over the island, straight and tall against a backdrop of mountains. I see it clearly for what it is; something to lean against, a place for me to catch my breath.

The next morning, the sun wakes me. I check my watch. 4:30 a.m. I lie still listening to the lack of wind, the lack of rain. Through the window, the sky is too blue, the mountains too clear. I have to get up. I slip out of bed careful not to disturb Kyle and climb the stairs to the room with the light. I sit on the wooden planks and take in what the day is offering. It is a different landscape under a blue sky; blurred lines are now sharp, moody dark stands of trees suddenly look like parks, the icy cold water looks swimmable. I smile back at the bright landscape as it shows off.

"There are usually only one or two of these days a summer," Kyle says from behind me. "It's worth the 363 days of rain, isn't it?"

I nod as he sits down next to me and wraps the gray blanket he has brought with him around us both. "Look at that." His eyes run across the long expanse of peaks and valleys and ice and water. "Doesn't it make you want to go out and explore it all?"

"Not really. I like to just look at it from here."

"How can you say that? Miles of bears and moose and glaciers—it would be so cool to check it all out."

I turn to my right, count the peaks, pick out the one that I have been running from. I study the long smooth glacier wrapped tightly around one side of it.

"I've spent a fair amount of time on that one there."

He follows my finger, looks down the channel to the south. "You climbed Candoa? I didn't know that. You never said-"

"No. Three peaks to the south of Candoa. It's called Knight Peak, named after some guy from Juneau who climbed it first. He also named the biggest glacier in the Juneau Ice Field after himself, the one that originates at the top of the Peak. The best access is from the other side of the Ice Field in BC."

Kyle raises his eyebrows. "When was this?"

"Three years ago now."

"Is there anything you don't do? Rock climbing, glaciers. Has National Geographic interviewed you?"

"One summer was enough out there."

"You are so sexy, let's go back to bed."

"I'm trying to say it wasn't good."

"I'm trying to say it's time to go back to bed. Nothing in Alaska is all good, except you."

The next morning, the rain is back. It beats against my shoulders through my raingear as we haul two loads of wood then get back to work on the greenhouse. My muscles are beginning to wrap tighter to bone with all the work and cold rain.

We finish building the structure, long and low to the ground and rounded on top, nothing the wind can get a hold of easily. As we drape the thick plastic that will become the walls over the structure, it takes both of us to hold it in place, to keep the wind from tearing it from our hands. When the plastic is battened down and secured, we step inside. There is just enough room to stand up straight in the middle. It feels like we are in a big caterpillar shaped tent, the wind blowing hard at one side.

"Should've made it a little taller," Kyle says, crouching to shave off a couple inches of height. I can stand up straight in the middle.

"If we can figure out a way to heat it, we could grow vegetables longer, maybe even all winter."

"I'll bet we can find a small woodstove at the dump that would keep it warm enough, at least for another few months."

That night I reorganize the kitchen cupboards, while Kyle continues his methodical survey of all the plastic containers in the shed. I light the two propane lanterns, ignoring the bad smell, figuring I'll get used to it.

Standing on the counter, I move extra cans of tomatoes, beans and corn to the top shelf which is too high to reach from the ground. The first can only slides in a few inches before it bumps up against something. My fingers probe the dark until they find cardboard. I pull out a small, open box. On top is an opened envelope. WILLIAM HARRIS, it says, c/o US COAST GUARD, HIBLER ROCK. I climb down from the counter and unfold the piece of paper inside.

January 14, 1978

Dear Mr. Harris,
    Our records show you have failed to register with us

since your return from service. Please fill out the attached form and return it to the address below.

Sincerely,

Jason Denegrue
US Veterans Administration
652 West State St.
Washington, DC 20420

I set the letter on the table. *William Harris,* I think. The form he was supposed to fill out and send in is still in the envelope. I pick up a leather belt next. It's deep brown, indented and smooth where the buckle spent years rubbing. There are a set of drawing pencils and a sketchpad. I open it to the first page and study the sketch of mountains and sea.

And then I recognize it.

I run the stairs into the room with the light and peer across the water from the vantage point of the desk. The angle of the peaks, the order of the valleys, match the drawing in my hand. I flip to the next sketch. It is just as detailed. I circle the room slowly until I find it. It's the sixth pane to the right of the desk. I hold his drawing up and compare it to the view in front of me. I study each angle, the pattern of the ice. The glaciers have grown looser on the sides and more deeply furrowed up top, but they are still recognizable. The deep shifting sounds glaciers make in the night comes back to me.

I swallow hard and flip to the third sketch. It's of the light-house itself rising large against a dark sky. The perspective is skewed so that it seems to hang overhead, about to topple over onto the viewer.

The fourth says SELF PORTRAIT in tight neat print at the top. I study it closely. The sketch is of vast water and stretching sky, nothing to fill the page except the rocky tail of the island separating the two. I recognize the rocks I've stood on at low tide.

"Are you supposed to be in here?" I ask William Harris just above a whisper. "Or is the point that you're not?"

In the bottom left corner of each sketch is a scribbled signature. I try to make out a W or an H, but it is neither.

I carry the sketchpad back to the kitchen table and rustle through the rest of the box. I find a receipt from Chugach Motors in Neely dated July 12, 1978, a couple of pens, a vice for tying flies and several baggies of feathers and colored string, and on the very bottom, a page torn from the sketchbook, which I pick up. The numbers are large and bold and shaded. He took his time, they are perfectly even, and have the quality of a typewriter. Kyle walks in.

"William Harris was his name."

Kyle stares.

"The guy who lived here before us," I add.

His eyes drop to the box on the table. "Where'd you find that?"

"On the top shelf up there."

He shifts carefully through the feathers and papers and picks up the belt. His belt sunk with everything else in the skiff. He examines it, turns it over in his hands before he slips it through his own empty belt loops. The tongue of the buckle slides into its usual place. It fits him, exactly. We both stare at his waist.

"Guess he was your size," I say.

Kyle is slow to respond. "Guess so." When he looks up he says, "Nothing like a dead guy's belt."

"Disappeared doesn't mean dead."

He notices the torn page in my hand, moves my thumb so that he can see clearly the bold arc of the 2 and the perfect shading of the 9. "Why was he so obsessed with the number 29?"

I shrug. "Seems like he was working through something."

"Or he was just fucking nuts."

"He was a vet," I say, pointing out the letter. Kyle glances at it, but doesn't pick it up. "And a good artist." I show him the drawings in the sketchbook which he flips through slowly.

"I feel bad for the guy. He must've been lonely out here by himself," I say.

"Why are you so interested in him?" Kyle asks.

"No one has chosen to live out here in the past twenty years except him and us. I just wonder who he was and why he chose this." *And if it helped him*, I think but do not say.

9.

BY THE third day out on the ice, the students had all mastered walking in crampons. I set a faster pace and everyone kept up. Jason hiked next to me, instead of at the back of the group, which was a slight breach of protocol for two guides. I thought about pointing it out, but liked the way his southern accent rounded out all of his stories. We compared notes on Utah, Colorado, and Arizona, who had climbed what. We had been in Joshua Tree within months of each other, in Ouray at the same time.

I took a few compass bearings and shifted our course to keep us on Brad's route. We entered an old drainage area that water had carved into a steep sloping wall of dense blue ice. It rose forty feet in the air off to our right. It was like hiking through the inside of a frozen wave. The color of the air changed as the blue rose above us. The students fell silent as they walked under the ceiling of ice. I watched them lose themselves, shed their self-conscious ticks in the face of something that cannot be judged, something that just is.

The silence enveloped Jason and me as well. He ran his hand along the smooth blue ice. When we came out the other side and headed up a slow incline, he said, "I've been looking forward to that spot ever since I pulled into town."

"Have you spent much time farther up the glacier?"

"No, just run this route for Brad a couple times. Most of my glacier time has been up in the Wrangell-St. Elias."

"It gets better and better the higher up you go. I'd like to get back up there after this trip. I need a partner."

"Did you just ask me out?"

"I asked you on a climbing trip. I just need somebody on the other end of the rope."

"Yes. I'll go out with you."

At that point, I realized I hadn't checked behind me in a while. Stephanie, the small twiggy girl, had fallen a hundred yards behind the rest of the group. Elizabeth, who had been at the front of the pack behind Jason and me, had turned around and was walking toward Stephanie.

"Hold up here," I said to Jason, then walked quickly toward the back of the group in long solid strides. But Elizabeth got to Stephanie before I was anywhere close.

Stephanie took a step back and studied Elizabeth with a guarded look while she spoke. Elizabeth slid out of her pack first, and then Stephanie did the same. Elizabeth began stuffing what she could of Stephanie's gear into the top of her own pack and then tied more to the outside. She lifted the overloaded pack to her knee first and then struggled to get it to her back. She stumbled to her left and almost went down, but she got her feet underneath her just as the weight evened out across her shoulders. Without another glance in Stephanie's direction, Elizabeth began the work of catching back up to the group that had gathered around Jason.

When he saw that all three of us were walking again, he got the rest of the group moving as well. I stayed in the back to make sure Stephanie didn't fall behind again. With a lighter pack, she was able to keep up. I watched Elizabeth slowly pass one person after the next until she had resumed her spot at the front of the line. For the rest of the day she remained bent toward the ice under a pack heavier than mine. I smiled as I watched her plant each foot solidly on the uneven surface of the ice.

Across the next two days, Elizabeth still under the weight of that heavy pack, set the pace and it was fast. She hiked on my heels, pushing my speed. The initial tension between Elizabeth and the rest of the group quickly dissipated, diluted by the rest of Elizabeth's actions. I watched her from afar, amazed at the ferocity with which she did everything. She never measured, just poured in everything that she had to accomplish whatever she had decided to do.

The group seemed to recognize Elizabeth as something other. They settled into two camps of equal numbers; those who were drawn to Elizabeth and those who didn't like her. The kids who didn't like her kept pace because they didn't want to be shown up, while the kids who admired her kept up as well, trying to be more like her. Even Stephanie kept up. Each morning, Elizabeth carried her pack over to Stephanie's tent and took what she could fit. The result was, we were half way through Brad's route in a little less than a week. I considered a day off, but the rain had moved in, a slow steady drizzle that was too cold to do anything in except move or be zipped up in a sleeping bag. I took another compass bearing, consulted the aerial photo.

We were a day and a half hike from a valley I'd discovered while out on the ice alone. It was an area that water had carved into a maze of twenty foot swirling blue statues that you could walk around and through. I thought about the reaction of the kids to the smaller valley we had walked through. They would be amazed by the one farther north. I looked over my shoulder at Jason who was moving toward me with the rest of the kids. I wanted to show him.

"Hold up," I said to Elizabeth. We hunched against the rain while we waited for everyone to catch up. The wind blew the sound of their crampons toward us long before they arrived. Once the group was assembled I said, "We're going to take a detour, head north for a while."

Jason looked up.

"Keep your eyes on the ice. You'll still be able to see the crevasses. Let's tighten up the pack a little."

As we got underway again, Jason stayed up front next to me.

"This isn't a good idea."

"It's fine. I spent weeks up here, we'll be well below the snow. There's something I want you to see."

He shook his head, but the look in his eye is what led me to sneak into his tent later that night.

"They still hate me," Elizabeth said after dinner, not achieving the nonchalance she was aiming for. It was my night to do dishes and she had volunteered to help. The wind flapped the sides of the cook tent and blew across our feet.

"I think most of them just can't figure you out."

"I can usually get boys to like me, but even that's not working. That prick Rob's probably been talking.

"It's always like this," she went on, "My Dad always points out how many people don't like me." She said it in an offhand way, but the look on her face was anything but flippant as she reached for another bowl to dry.

I turned to face her in the dim light of the cook tent. "Is it bad at home?" It seemed to me there were two ways to end up if that was the situation, like her or like me, a raging river or a series of locks.

The bowl she was drying fell still. "My dad says some really mean shit and my mom pretends like it's fine. It's not fine. And then comes the long periods where I might as well be invisible." Without looking up she said, "They think I'm a bad person."

"A bad person wouldn't have carried most of Stephanie's gear for the last week."

"She's so little."

"She is little, but that doesn't mean you have to carry her gear. Everyone is responsible for themselves."

Elizabeth twisted the bowl in her hands.

"Don't let your parents convince you of anything. You're way more capable than you get credit for, especially from yourself.

"You'll be graduated this time next year," I said. "I never went home again after I graduated from high school."

"I don't think I can make it that long." She tightened her grip on the bowl, tapped it twice against the flat of one hand. "My father introduced me to his girlfriend. Christie. As if I wouldn't know. As if I didn't notice the way his hand dropped when he held the door open for her. He might as well have just grabbed her ass. I told my mom and she won't do shit about it. Do you know what she said? 'Christie's been a good friend for a long time.'" Elizabeth rolled her eyes, gaining speed. "Are you kidding me? Christie works at my dad's office so I called her up, said I really wanted to see her again. I think she thought we would bond or something."

"She agreed to meet you?"

Elizabeth made a dramatic face and nodded.

"What an idiot."

"She's an even bigger loser than he is. I told her I thought it was only fair that she know about everything—that she was my dad's girlfriend but that she wasn't the only one. We'd been at a picnic a couple weekends before—my parents and me. I took a picture of him with my friend's mom who's really hot. He was doing that thing that he always does with attractive women where he leans toward them a little when they're talking and tilts his head. He gets this look on his face like he thinks whatever they are saying is the most interesting thing in the world. It's sickening. Anyway, you should've seen Christie's face when I showed her the picture. I told her I was sure he'd deny it but that he was a liar anyway, I mean, he already had to lie to my mom about both girlfriends, how hard would it be to lie about one to the other? And if there were two, didn't that mean there could be three or four—maybe one of them is just a weekend fuck—and how many one night stands are there?"

"That's why they sent you here?"

"My mom is pathetic." Elizabeth dropped her head, rubbed at her eyes. "Why won't she stand up to him? She invited Christie to their anniversary party. A huge stupid party to celebrate twenty amazing years, so that everyone can continue to think everything is perfect." Elizabeth looked up, her hair pulling out of a braid, her eyes red. "They sent me here because I snuck a bunch of champagne and instead of giving the toast I was supposed to, I said all that."

I raised my eyebrows. "You told an entire room full of people that your Dad was sleeping with Christie?"

"Yeah." Elizabeth looked down again.

"Did you say the part about the weekend fuck?"

Elizabeth nodded, a pained look on her face. "All of it. And then I threw up. I am a bad person."

Despite everything I know about working with kids, I laughed. I laughed until I had to sit down. Elizabeth just stared at me at first and then she started laughing also.

"That is awesome." I wiped at my eyes, started laughing again. "You're braver than I am. I just took it all those years with my head down. Maybe you're right, maybe you can't stay, they sound awful. You're going to be just fine once you get out into the world on your own. You're not a bad person, you've just got a lot of fire in you. That might be your greatest asset." I picked up the last few dishes and dropped them in with the melted chunk of glacier that was now cold dishwater. I glanced over at Elizabeth and added, "And you're hilarious."

The day we hiked due north, the clouds cleared and the sun came out. By noon, it was hot enough to strip down to a t-shirt. The division between glacier and sky was a sharp thin line far ahead of us. Everyone's spirits soared in the warmth. Elizabeth hiked next to me, even faster than usual, everyone else in a line behind us. She sang the lyrics and danced under her heavy pack to some repetitive hip hop song about how rich and famous some guy was.

"Could you maybe sing something more annoying?" I asked after the fourth or fifth time through.

She launched into something much worse about trailer park girls. I groaned.

"Why is it that all adults hate good music?" She asked.

"I'm not really an adult. And that's not good music."

"Well you're not a parent, but you're an adult. I mean, you're in charge of all of us." She gestured toward the long line of kids behind us and then turned back to me. "What's wrong with your parents, anyway?"

"I don't want to talk about my parents."

"That's great. Just keep it all bottled up inside. That seems to work well for my mother. What was wrong with them? Did they get drunk and beat on each other?"

"Stop it."

Elizabeth stepped in front of me, stopping me short. "C'mon Anna! Let it out!"

We faced off, the sun bright between us. Her eyes hot and fluid, mine cold and still. "Like this," she said. She waited, seemed to let everything gather and then closed her eyes, dropped her head back and let out a scream that filled in all the space between glacier and sky. It pushed against the blood in my veins, making it move faster. I wanted to stop her, contain what she was letting spill out, but I couldn't move. When it was over, she caught my eye again and smiled, then began to spin, her arms out wide, three, four revolutions until her crampon caught on the ice and tripped her.

She lay like a turtle on its back, still strapped into her heavy pack. She kicked her legs a couple times and leaned hard to the left trying to roll over. She tried to unbuckle the strap at her waist, but there was too much tension on it.

"Anna?" she said as calmly as if she'd just knocked on a door and was wondering if I was in the room. She kicked and flailed some more, trying hard to roll onto her side, which made us both start laughing.

She reached up a hand. I put both of mine on my hips as

I stood over her. "Anna! Come on! You gotta help me! I can't get up! Only ugly people hold a grudge!" She kicked again, this time catching the ice with her crampon. She made it to her hands and knees. I grabbed her by the pack and hauled her to her feet. "Thanks," she said, wiping her wet hands on her thighs. She glanced over her shoulder at me. "I was just trying to help you."

"I don't need the help."

"Yes you do." She glanced back at how much distance the rest of the group had closed between us and them then started off again, in order to maintain her position at the front.

I kept the aerial photo out on which I had marked the two big crevasses, to make sure we hiked clear of them. Jason kept the back of the group close to the front, so that no one could wander off the path I set.

That afternoon, we took a break.

"I don't want one," Elizabeth said when I handed out thin blank journals to all the kids.

"Take one," I said, "It'll be a place where you can write down what's going on for you."

"I don't like to write."

I dropped a journal in her lap.

While the other kids wrote and pondered and wrote some more, perched on their backpacks on the ice, Elizabeth left her journal closed. She stared at the sky and picked at her fingernails. Eventually she opened it, bent over a single page somewhere in the middle, and tapped her pen against her lower lip before finally writing something quickly. I noticed my name when I walked by. She'd printed: *Anna is my only friend out here.* The last two words were crossed through, the period moved.

The next afternoon we walked into the valley of ice sculptures. It was a narrow valley, carved by water long ago. The smooth blue walls of ice rose one hundred yards apart, on either side of us. When the water had receded, what was left were the hardest, most dense parts of the glacier. The flow of water had pulled away with it anything of lesser strength. I walked past one that was six feet high, two feet wide, swirled and tall like a dancer in motion. Elizabeth stopped in front of another. A wide angular top attached by the narrowest pencil of ice to a thick, perfectly smooth round column. She kept her eye on the pencil part at shoulder level, walking past it carefully. The silence that gripped all of us when we first entered the valley soon turned into a collective giddiness at being in a secret place like no other on earth. We set up camp and spent all afternoon there, exploring.

I laughed at the boys who climbed up the sloping valley wall and slid down on their backs. "Careful," I said. "Not going to be pretty if you catch a crampon."

Elizabeth sat down next to me, the valley spreading out ahead of us. "I never really imagined there were actually places like this," she said. "I mean, you see them on tv, but to see it for yourself is totally different. There must be a thousand places like this to go to in the world."

"There are."

"And a thousand people to meet who don't know anything about your parents or what they think of you or who you are when you're with them."

"Exactly," I said.

That night in Jason's tent, we made plans for the fall and winter, both of us zipped into his sleeping bag. Rock climbing in Arizona until the snow flew and then on to the ice in Ouray.

It took us a day and a half to backtrack to the original route. Elizabeth hiked along next to me, but didn't talk much. Once we were back on Brad's route, I checked the aerial photo for the location of the nearest crevasse and took us wide around it. We set up camp against an ice wall that blocked the wind nicely. I set up my tent, unrolled my sleeping bag, waited until all the kids were sleeping and then snuck over to Jason's tent, as I had each night since the valley of sculptures.

The next morning, I meant to be up before everyone else to sneak back to my tent, but heard a few stirrings, and so went straight to the cook tent and got breakfast going.

Jason came in right after me. "Did you leave your tent open?" he asked in a low voice, so the kids wouldn't hear.

"No," I said, pulling the bubbling oatmeal off the camp stove.

"Oh shit, we might've been busted." He made a face that suggested he didn't really care.

The kids were milling around outside the cooktent. "Grab your bowl and spoon," I said. "Breakfast is ready."

As everyone gathered around and I scooped oatmeal into bowls, I noticed Elizabeth wasn't up yet. I asked Natalie, her tentmate, to go tell her breakfast was ready.

"She wasn't there when I woke up. I thought she got up early." Natalie said.

I looked at each of the faces, now turned toward me, to see what I would do. "Is she in anyone else's tent?"

"I wish," said one of the older boys. Some of the other boys snickered quietly. Everyone else shook their heads.

Jason stood up. I watched him scan the horizon for a second before I allowed myself to start doing the same. The kids held still, watching both of us intently. "Stay here," I said to them, as I crossed the ice quickly to Elizabeth and Natalie's tent.

Her boots were gone, her sleeping bag, and the top of her pack that could be worn as a small backpack. As I stood up in the cold wind, I felt the back of my throat closing. I combed the ice for footprints around the tent, small knicks in the ice from crampons, the indentation of a slight slide. Whatever had been there, the wind had smoothed over. I could barely swallow as my mind raced in every direction.

In the cooktent, I tore through the food bags. She'd taken

enough for two or three days. If she hiked straight down the glacier, she'd be back in town in two to four days depending on how much she hiked at night.

The kids huddled in front of the cooktent, looking stricken. "Pack up your gear, I'm going to call for the helicopter. They'll find her." I said and then ran to my own tent. The door was indeed unzipped and flapping. The satellite phone was in the top of my pack in a ziplock bag. It was cold, slow to turn on, even slower to find enough satellites to work. As I sat on my knees in my tent bent over the phone, I noticed my sleeping bag looked slept in.

The connection was bad, but I eventually made Brad understand that he needed to hire a helicopter to fly the length of the glacier to find Elizabeth.

There were two major crevasses between us and town. The night before had been dark and overcast. All it would take is one misstep.

Jason and I did not talk as we hiked the group at just under a run to the first crevasse she would've come to.

Instead of her usual place near the back, Stephanie hiked next to me. I could feel her hostility. When I finally looked over at her she said, "Elizabeth needed you last night, she was upset, but you were in Jason's tent."

We were at the crevasse before I could recover or even register what she meant. The ground fell away in a jagged line one hundred fifty feet long and forty feet wide. Jason gathered the students a safe distance away while I stepped into a harness and dug ropes out of the bottom of my pack avoiding everyone's eyes. Jason and I worked fast, setting gear, tying in. I would drop over the edge since I was lightest, he would stay on the surface, help pull me, or her, out if necessary. The helicopter beat through the air, echoed off the mountains, getting closer and eventually landing on the ice not far from where the kids sat in a tight group. I stood at the lip of the chute, while Jason double checked knots and anchors.

Brad crossed the ice, low to avoid the still turning blades. I watched him gather the three closest students and motion for them to follow him back to the helicopter. He turned to me as they stood up and shook his head once. They hadn't seen her. I snapped the line I was tied into and farther up on the ice, Jason snapped back. I stepped off the edge and dropped inside the body of the glacier.

10.

THE NEXT morning the wind blows so hard through the channel I swear I can feel the top of the lighthouse sway.

"Guess going to town is out." Kyle is half dressed, peering through the upstairs window.

"There's always wood to split." I prop myself on one elbow in the bed.

"I wanted to go into town today." He peers down the channel in that direction.

"We might as well get used to not being able to get to town. It's only going to get worse in the next few months."

"That Coast Guard guy doesn't know what he's talking about. He's been riding a desk too long. We'll be able to be out in the skiff most of the winter."

"I don't think so." I roll on to my back.

He turns quickly to face me, eyes narrowed. "What do you know about being out on the water?"

I throw the covers off, pull on a heavy sweater and thick socks, ignoring him. He turns from the window and heads downstairs without a glance or another word.

He is outside by the time I come down the stairs. I shuffle through the box of William Harris' things looking for the sketchpad and pencils. I plan to spend the morning, perhaps the day, somewhere Kyle is not. Through the window I see him down on the beach, freeing the haulout line of seaweed. I pour myself some coffee and head upstairs.

I'd never done anything more than small sketches of wildflowers in my journal, once a detailed rendition of an ice cream sundae that I craved for the entirety of a two month backpacking trip.

One hour after another slips away as I sit at the desk that I have dragged over in front of pane number three, tentatively trying to recreate the inconsistencies of rock, the shallow tilt of valleys. I erase as much as I draw. At some point in the morning, I flip to William's sketch, compare the steadiness of his hand to the steadiness of my own.

I spend the afternoon splitting and stacking wood. Kyle stays in the shed. The wind pulls at everything in its way. I wait for Kyle to return to me. He does not.

The next morning, the weather is the same. I watch the waves pile up on each other, steep and chaotic. While I make dinner that night, he shuffles around under the stairs, moving things, then moving them back. He goes outside, splits a few pieces of wood and then comes back inside and sits down. When he stands up half a minute later, I turn around.

"Would you just pick something to do and do it?"

The muscles in his neck strain. "I can't focus. This fucking wind and there's no cove to tuck into or next bay to head for where it might be better."

I study his face. "It'll pass through in a couple days. You just need to relax."

He turns and walks up the stairs. I hear the trapdoor fall closed behind him.

The wind beats up the channel the next day as well. I split wood in the morning then spend the rest of the day up in the room with the light, sketching. Kyle stays in the shed until late in the afternoon when he goes for a walk. I watch his slow steps as he traces the perimeter of the island, far below me, hands in his pockets, eyes searching the horizon.

The next morning, it's perfectly calm. "See?" I say, watching him peer out the window when we first wake up.

"C'mon," he says. "We're getting out of here." He jumps out of bed and pulls clothes on.

The first thing we do is take showers at the harbor. There are two individual metal shower rooms for use by people living on boats or for anyone else who needs one. Seven minutes of water perfectly adjusted for temperature for five quarters. I wash and shampoo in a hurry and then stand in the powerful stream of water not wanting it to end. *Ten quarters,* I think to myself, *bring ten quarters next time.*

We find the truck in the harbor parking lot where we paid a small fee to be able to leave it. On the drive out to the greenhouse, I turn to face him. "Are we going to talk about it?"

"What?"

"The last couple days?"

"It's fine."

"It didn't seem fine."

"It's fine." He looks at me for the first time since we left the lighthouse that morning. I see in his face the plea to let it go, to just stand close while he figures it out on his own, and I recognize it for what I am asking him to do.

At the greenhouse, I buy ten bags of dirt and compost along with mostly-grown peppers, lettuce, spinach, broccoli, beets and squash. While a teenage boy carefully packs them into boxes for the ride back out, the man who owns the greenhouse says, "Aren't you the new lighthouse people?"

A specific feeling lands in my chest, burns there, bright for a minute. An identity. A good one.

We drive to the dump next, pay the guy in the building five dollars to be allowed to search through the mountains of junk. He tells us he's seen a couple woodstoves in the far northwest corner. We walk the dirt pathways between hills of rusty junk until we get to the one that supposedly has some woodstoves in it. Kyle climbs the mountain, sliding on old bikes and deflated buoys with each foot step. I start at the edge of the pile where it meets the ground. I do not find a woodstove, instead I get tangled in an old fishing net.

Farther up the pile, Kyle moves a refrigerator door and uncovers a small stove that's missing its door. "This will work," he calls down. "Now we just need a door." After another hour, we find a door that is too big, but will work. We stop by the hardware store on the way back, pick up bailing wire to attach the door to the stove, charcoal, and some seeds to start to see if we can coax them through the winter.

The next four days out at the lighthouse hold absolutely still. The first day we haul five loads of wood. The next two days, seven each. The fourth day, we push it to eight. There is a mountain of wood on our beach. When the wind starts on the fifth day, we begin hauling the wood up to the house to split. We work side by side, Kyle's ax swings and then mine, under clear blue skies. My shoulders ache audibly. I fall into the rhythm of the work, the shape of the day. I imagine William Harris standing where I am, doing the same thing. He got to the end of one lease, and signed up for another. I see each month ahead of us rolling into the next, imagine signing my name again.

On the fifth day, the wind begins to make up for lost time. We are forced to switch to inside chores. I build a hobbit door for the greenhouse with some scrap two by fours and the rest of the plastic, while Kyle installs the stove and the stovepipe that will carry the smoke out. He reinforces it with wood so that it won't melt the plastic. I'm not entirely convinced it won't still melt the plastic. Kyle secures the door to the stove with the bailing wire so that it only hangs a little bit crooked. "Hope plants don't mind a little smoke," he says.

"It will be a freaking miracle if anything grows out here." I look at the peppers and squash and other veggies, growing in five gallon buckets that I found in the shed and drilled holes in. To water them, I carry each bucket out to the cistern and set them down under the spigot. There is plenty of water now. I bang on the side to make sure. It is hard and full under my fist as high as I can reach.

After a solid week of wind and sideways rain, Kyle and I are both in the room with the light. He's behind me tinkering with the moving parts. I'm standing, hands against the thick pane of glass. I start where I always start, on the east edge of the easternmost window and begin to move my eyes west. I follow the peaks, the valleys, the smooth lines of the glaciers that I can make out through the hazy cloud cover. I close my eyes and start over, recreating each angle in my mind. I know the edges of ice, the steepness of rock, the jagged line of valleys as well as I know the details of my own history. I think about picking up the sketchpad, but decide against it. I imagine William Harris standing where I am and wonder if being out here made him worse or better.

"Looks like I can't get to town today either," Kyle says standing up. We've split all the wood. My hands are thick with calluses.

He begins putting his tools back into the toolbox. I hear metal thrown against metal.

I turn to face him. "It's supposed to break tomorrow."

"Yeah." He picks up his toolbox and steps past me. "Tomorrow."

Later that afternoon, I watch him walk the edge of the island, far below me, hands in his pockets. The wind has blown itself out, is only a strong, steady breeze. I decide to join him. There has to be something to say to turn him back toward me.

As I cross the highest point of the island, the halibut fisherman's skiff comes into view. He's closer to the island this time. The man turns the skiff as if he might head toward our beach, but then backs off the throttle and floats. I follow his gaze to Kyle on the rocks below me. Kyle has stopped, is staring back. I see the anger in the way he stands. If there were not water between them, I imagine Kyle would run at the man, chase him off. Slow seconds pass before the man swings the skiff around and begins the process of setting his fishing gear.

Kyle's cheeks are flushed. His eyes are sharp. I reach for his hand but it is balled into a fist. "What the fuck is that guy doing?"

"He's just some dude that doesn't know how to halibut fish." I try to catch Kyle's eye but he's still watching the man as he drops his buoys over and then the long line with hooks.

"He's throwing his gear in exactly the same place where he didn't catch anything last time. What a fucking idiot. And what was that business?" He flings his arm in the direction of the water where the guy was before he began setting gear.

"I don't know. It's a little weird," I agree.

"A little?" Kyle walks off and I don't follow.

* * * *

Over the next four weeks, the weather fights with itself. There are fewer and fewer days we can get off the island. Every one of them must be spent cutting and hauling firewood. Every break from the rain must be spent painting the lighthouse. Town starts to feel farther and farther away. I find myself peering in that direction more often, reminding myself that it's still there.

Late one night, while sitting at the small desk in the room with the light, I flip to William's drawings at the front of the sketchpad. Somehow, he has made the mountains look exactly as they do when the weather moves in from the north. There is not a stray line on the page. Every mark adds something to the whole. I study the signature in the bottom corner, again try to make out a W or an H in the scribble, but can't.

I set the pad down on the small desk and stare out the window. There are the peaks of the mountains that drop into the ocean in the foreground and then another set behind those. I study the set of peaks in the distance, the uneven treeline of the first, the way the second and third hide part of the fourth. My eyes drop to the signature again. It's an exact replica.

I understand William Harris perfectly in that moment. The desire to be made out of something more substantial, something that can be altered by the wind, but not torn apart by it.

The Styrofoam I packed into the window where I ran the water hose starts to whistle when the wind blows. Glancing in the direction of the noise one night, I say, "We'll need something else come winter."

Kyle looks up from the loose pieces of the Evinrude he's taken apart, spread across the kitchen table and floor. He drops his eyes as soon as they meet mine, shifts in his seat, says nothing. It is as though he has not, or will not, consider a winter out here. A hot dread fills me, lava turning to stone. *Would I stay out here alone?* I do not breathe, wait for him to say something that will displace it.

Instead, he bends over the small piece of machinery in his hand.

Two days later, I wake to a perfect calm that I can sense before I see. I sit up in bed, peer out the window to make sure. The ocean is as smooth and flat as I've ever seen it. I watch Kyle still sleeping next to me and smile knowing how happy he'll be. Before I wake him, before we rush out the door, I breathe deep the strength of the lighthouse, the lack of wind, the ability to be still.

I bend down, kiss the smooth skin of Kyle's neck. "C'mon," I say when he stirs. "We're going to town."

As soon as we set foot on the dock in Neely, Kyle's spirits soar. I shake my head and smile back at his wide grin. Without the sound of the outboard between us, I can finally ask, "What else do you want to do besides go to the grocery store?" I feel in my pocket to make sure I still have the grocery list. It isn't long yet, nothing on it of dire importance.

I watch him glance up at the buildings of town from our lower vantage point on the docks. "I don't know. I saw a bathtub at the dump when we were out there. That'd be nice, wouldn't it?"

"Are you kidding? That'd be great."

We head down the long dirt driveway to the dump, pay the guy in the small building five dollars again and wind our way through the mountains of junk.

Kyle relocates the tub while I'm distracted by the wrecked cars. A clawfoot with two feet missing and a large caulked crack through the middle.

"Perfect." I run my hand along the top rim, test it to see how heavy it is.

The men at the dump help us lift it into the back of the truck. I'm heading for the passenger door when Kyle asks the younger of the two men, "How's it been going around here?"

"Pretty good," he says, sliding his hands into his pockets. The other man, standing closer to me, leans both his elbows on the bed of the truck. We don't know each other necessarily, but we all recognize each other.

"Fishing gotten any better?" Kyle asks.

"Hell no," the older man says. "Those guys are spending all season in the bar."

"It's a bad one," the younger guy agrees. "How's it going out there? You guys are at the lighthouse, right?"

"Yeah," Kyle says. "It's good. Real good."

I watch him nod one too many times.

* * * *

The tub is too heavy to lift with each of us on a side, so we have to pick up one side at a time together to get it in and out of the skiff and up to the house.

"Here would be nice," I say breathing hard between the two trees. The branches start about ten feet over my head.

We shimmy the tub into place.

Kyle finds wood to stack up under the missing feet while I get the stove going to heat water. I find three pieces of Styrofoam in the shed that I tape together, then cut to fit snugly over the top of the tub. After each bucket of water is added, I replace the Styrofoam to keep the heat in.

Late in the afternoon, I slide into the warm water, the branches overlapping above me. I decide that I like the looseness of it, the way light is allowed in, a tolerance of sky by the trees. The tub leaks some, but not fast and I don't notice the crack in the bottom as long as I don't slide over it. I feel my muscles let go their tight hold of my bones, my brain let go its tight hold on everything.

Behind me, I hear Kyle holler, catch sight of his naked body as he sprints through the light drizzle. I laugh as he splashes into the tub, wrapping his body tight against mine.

* * * * *

When the chatter on the radio begins to include coho salmon, I clean out the small smokehouse and scrub down all the racks. It's a simple structure, about as tall and wide as a person, with six metal shelves. The slow, smoky fire burns in a metal bucket with holes punched in it to allow air. On the next calm morning, three days later, we collect green alder in addition to the usual three boatloads of firewood.

A week passes before we are able to go anywhere again. We continue to paint and shuffle scaffolding on the less windy side of the house until finally, the wind dies. With fishing poles and the beer we've been saving, we take the skiff over to the nearest stream the cohos run up.

We beach the skiff and I sink the beers in the cold river water. "Hey bears!" I yell up the alder tunneled stream corridor, thrilled to be off the island, if only for a couple hours.

Kyle walks up behind me with both fishing rods. His eyes lock on the surface of the water. It is one dark mass underneath, fish stacked up in that final desperate push upstream. His hood is off, the rain gathers on his hair. His hands are red with the cold.

"It's thick," he says. "Looks like the cohos are going to make up for the rest of the shitty season." He squints, tries to see under the surface better. "Everybody's making money, now." A look that I've not seen before passes over his face. He hands me one of the rods and heads upstream, whistling in loud sharp blasts while clapping his hands. The brush crashes wildly on the opposite shore. Kyle freezes and I look up in time to see the back end of a black bear running away.

With my first cast, I reel in a chum salmon, not good eating unless you're a bear or an eagle. I work the hook out of the back of the foot long fish and toss him back.

I snag two more chums before I catch the first coho. I knock it in the head with a rock until it stops moving. I lay its silver body on the rocks and cast again. In a little over an hour, there are five fish, ten to twelve pounds each laid out on the beach next to me. The wind has returned, is beginning to push at my back. I glance out at the water, watch it toss and turn.

I hear feet against river rocks far upstream. I listen, try to distinguish a pattern. Four feet or two? I glance at my line of fish, laid out on the rocks, hear the interested eagles that have gathered overhead. I take two steps backward, toward the skiff and peer upstream. The steps are louder, all sliding rocks. Nothing to distinguish. I should holler but instead fear coats my throat as I picture the bear that will appear from around the edge of brush at any moment. The unpredictability. The number of pounds by which I am outweighed. He will go for the fish. Or will he go for me? Should I hide behind the skiff? Should I stand my ground? My mind races as I try to recognize myself. When did I become so afraid of what could happen to me?

Kyle appears around the corner, a black bag full of salmon thrown over his shoulder. The fear drains, pools at my feet, but does not leave entirely. When I look up at Kyle's face, the fear surges. I am afraid of what is happening to him, of whatever happened to William Harris. I know suddenly and clearly that we need to leave the lighthouse for Kyle's sake and that we need to stay for mine.

11.

THAT AFTERNOON, I begin the work of smoking and canning the salmon. It is the last week of September. We've only ever seen the beginning of October in Alaska and never a November. I fillet each fish and prepare the salty sweet brine. I slice each fillet into long thin strips that will soak overnight in every pot and pan in the house. It makes me feel rich, this much meat. This much preparing for what's to come. I had the same feeling watching the wood pile grow, our combined efforts producing future heat and food. This is where it starts, I tell myself. This is how to rebuild trust in myself, in life, in the way of things, by investing in something, one small task at a time.

Early the next morning Kyle is up and moving around. I hear him making coffee and check my watch. It's just before five. I pull on clothes and move down the stairs.

When he sees me, he pours a cup of hot coffee for me. The fire pops in the cookstove.

"It's calm out. I'm going to town. Want to come?" He asks as he hands me the steaming mug with just the right amount of milk.

I glance around the room at all the fish soaking.

"We'll be back by noon," he says. "I'm sure the wind will pick up by then anyway."

"What do we need?" I ask, thinking of the showers. Seven minutes of relaxing warmth.

"I ordered some supplies to build a kayak last time I was in town."

I raise my eyebrows, hold his gaze over my coffee mug. "You did?"

"I've always wanted to build one, the kind the natives used. I found a book out in the shed a while back. The whole thing is tied together so that it flexes in the waves." His eyes are bright and animated for the first time in a long time. "They took them out in the worst weather. I thought it'd be good to have a project for the winter."

I nod my agreement, caught between happiness at his mention of a winter out here, and trepidation that what he will spend the winter building is the one thing that will get us off the island. "I'll get dressed."

The wind is already bad by 9am. I have to skip the shower. I grocery shop quickly, grabbing three of everything, feeling like we will not be back for a long time.

Kyle is loading boxes of kayak supplies in the skiff when I get down to the harbor. The sea between us and the lighthouse is a million steep mountains. The van from the grocery store pulls up behind me and Kyle and I work quickly to get the food packed into the skiff. The wind whips my hair into my face as he tosses me my float coat and pulls on his own.

I watch the chaotic motion of the boat against the dock, wait for the right moment to step in, then untie the bowline as I work to keep my balance. I pull my chin into the thick collar of my float coat as Kyle pulls out of the harbor and the sea opens up. I keep my weight low, hold onto either side of the caprail to decrease the tossing. Kyle keeps his head ducked against the rain that is thrown at us sideways as the Evinrude laboriously pushes us up each swell before we slide down the backside.

He opens up the throttle at one point, but the smacking of the hull is too much and he has to back off. Two hours stretch into three as rain runs down my neck and salt spray coats my face and neck and eyes. There is so much water, dark and moving. My fingers go numb wrapped tightly around the caprail.

When I glance back at Kyle's face, I see what I already know, that we should not be out here.

My eyes linger on the water. I tell myself it is not reaching for us.

We're tossed for another three hours before finally the lighthouse grows to its full size and our beach comes into view. I am stiff and numb, long past shivering. When I finally step over the bow, relief floods my body. I cannot wait to be inside building a fire, finding something to eat, while the weather rages on separate from me.

We carry the limp, wet boxes of food in. It all stays between us: the depth of the water, the way the force of the wind increases almost daily now, how town is slipping farther and farther out of reach. We don't talk as Kyle fills the cooler with food, while I put cans and chips and crackers away.

That afternoon, he disappears into the shed with his boat building supplies. I tear up alder branches and get a fire going in the smokehouse. I fill the racks with salmon, dripping with brine, slide them into place and close the door. A rich smoke seeps out the top and through all the cracks in the sides. Rather than increase throughout the afternoon as it usually does, the wind is losing power and the clouds are dropping.

I pack the rest of the brined fish in the coolers, then head out to the shed to see what Kyle is doing. The table saw starts up when I'm halfway between the lighthouse and the shed. Through the propped open double doors, I can see him pushing a long piece of wood through the spinning blade. He doesn't notice when I step inside. Lying on the workbench is a large roll of waxy looking cloth and several spools of nylon thread.

I wander over to where a book, slightly yellowed, is held open by a rock stretching across both pages. On the left hand page is a blueprint of a kayak cut in half and hollowed out. On the opposite page is text explaining the exact cuts: width, length and diameter of every rib, every crossbar. I think about what he said, *they took them out in the worst weather.* How far, I wonder, but I know, the Aleuts were gone from home for weeks at a time. I remember paintings I'd seen in Neely of native men, two to a kayak, wrapped in bear skins, their paddles in perfect unison as the sea screams all around them. I think of all the salmon I am smoking, how many jars it will fill, how I am putting up food to last all winter.

The saw stops behind me. Kyle lays a long strip of wood on the ground. "I found a whole stash of yellow cedar." He points at the stacked lumber against the north wall. "That's what the Aleuts used. They hunted whales from these things!"

"Where'd you get this book?"

"Found it in one of the plastic tubs." He checks the dimension of the piece on the floor with a tape measure.

"Have you gone through all of them?"

"Most of them."

I start to ask what's in them, but Kyle starts the saw up. I move over to one row of tubs stacked along the wall. I pull the top off of one. Inside are two 1960's style life vests, held together at the sides with what looks like shoe lace. US COAST GUARD is stamped on the back in faded block letters. I put the top back, slide the tub off the stack and look in the next one.

The second box is a mess of wires, rusted tools, dirty rags, pens, an old pair of rubber boots with holes at the ankles, an extension cord, a small blackened cook pot, several screws and wingnuts. I put the lid back on, slide the tub onto the ground and sit down on it as I pry the lid off the one on the bottom of the stack.

I find a neat row of the brown lighthouse logs, packed in tightly with spines up. I pull one from the middle. Stamped onto the front is US COAST GUARD HIBLER ROCK. The same as the one in the room with the light and the same as the blank books I found under the stairs. I open to the first page:

February 1963–June 1964
Tom Jordan, USCG, Petty Officer
Greg Phillips, USCG, Petty Officer

The entries on the following pages are in a long cursive, each no more than a line or two:

February 3, 1963 2123 Wind NNW 25 knots. *Chilkoot* radioed as they passed to say they were on their way to Juneau. Were advised winds are to increase.

February 7, 1963 0610 Wind SW 15 knots. *Jennifer Dawn* not under her own power, radioed to say they did not need help.

I flip through the pages, opened to one toward the end:

April 9, 1964 1459 Winds NE 30 knots. Northbound ferry passing.

The saw spins behind me. I slide the log back into place and pull out the one tucked against the side of the tub at the end of the row. The outside bears the same stamp.

I open it up. The date on the first page is April 1977–Sept 1979.

Underneath the date in small neat print it reads:

William Harris

Kyle's back is to me. I tuck the logbook under my arm and step out into the rain. The fog has closed in so that I can't make out either shore across the channel. I add more alder to the smokehouse fire, then flip the breaker labeled FOGHORN.

I jump when a deep three second bellow tumbles down the channel. Sound, in the absence of sight.

Inside, I make myself a sandwich and climb the stairs to the room with the light.

The world below me is a billowing hazy gray. I sit down on the wooden platform, tuck into a corner of glass and open to page one.

Instead of wind speed and boats passing, in careful, tight script is written:

September 10, 1977   1700   The generator has been down for five days. The weather's been bad for three weeks but I still like it out here. This is when they said it would get hard but I like the way the fog fills up the channel.

"So do I." I glance out the window into the haze. The foghorn sounds. I cannot see much of the sea beyond the edges of the island. My eyes rest on the roof of the shed. I hear the faint whine of the table saw, picture the pressure of Kyle's fingers against wood. I think of us taking our place, if a little shaky, in a line of lighthouse keepers. I think about this conversational, almost journal entry in an official Coast Guard logbook and recognize William Harris' loneliness on a new level.

I get up when I notice the smokehouse is barely smoking. Outside, I open the door and peer in. The alder pieces I added are too big and are not burning well. I grab another branch from the woodshed and whittle a pile of small chips with my knife until there are several handfuls to toss into the fire. I pull the chopping block over for a seat and whittle the rest of the long alder branches into a large pile of chips. In the absence of wind, the fog closes in tighter. I work to the pace set by the foghorn: This much done in thirty seconds, this much more done in one minute.

When the pile is more than a foot deep, I stand up and stretch my back. I pull my hand inside my sleeve so that I can move the racks around inside the smokehouse without getting burned. The salmon smells of wet earth, brown sugar and smoke.

Closing up the smokehouse, I walk over to the shed. On the floor next to the saw are four piles of different length pieces of wood. Kyle is studying the book, sawdust clings to his clothes and hair.

He turns as the foghorn sounds, waits until it finishes. "What are you up to?"

"I need a bucket for wood chips."

"Can you help me for a second?"

"Sure."

"I'm ready to cut the four longest pieces. I need you to hold one end."

"Alright."

As I support the long hanging end of a two by four, Kyle lines it up on the saw. He starts the blade and the sound of it fills up all the space in the shed. I wait until he begins to push the wood into the saw, and then slowly put forward pressure on my end of the wood, keeping it lined up, matching his progress.

"Stop!" Kyle yells over the spinning blade, pulling the wood quickly back toward himself, which makes me lose my grip. The wood bounces hard against the flat part of the table saw. I just barely catch my end before it hits the floor. "You're pushing too hard!" he yells. "You're going to make the cut crooked." His face is pinched in annoyance.

"Sorry." I mouth the word rather than say it.

He lines up again and I hold the end of the wood steady. As he leans forward, I match the pressure he puts on his end with pressure at my end.

"Anna!" he yells. "Jesus." He pushes the wood out of the way of the saw again and stops the blade. "Nevermind." He slides the wood roughly out of my hands and balances it against the workbench. "I'll just figure it out on my own."

He rushes around getting the sawhorses set how he wants them, stacking things on top to make them the same height as my hands had been.

I stand there stupidly as he balances the two by four, lines it up again and starts the blade. He spreads his arms as wide as they'll go to push evenly on both sides of the wood which puts his face inches from the surface of the table saw. The blade tears into the wood and I squint into the high pitched whine as he pushes the wood through, craning his neck to keep his head out of the way of the spinning blade.

I turn, pick up the bucket I came in for and head toward the door. I look back just before it closes behind me to see him inspecting the perfect cut he just made on his own.

For dinner, I cook everything that needs to be eaten first. I make a green salad and manage to cook a chicken in the woodstove, along with roasted veggies. Kyle seems not to have even noticed the fog, the way it has closed us in, or the way our interaction in the shed has closed me in. He speaks only of the kayak.

"It's called a bidarka. The Aleuts made twine out of dried animal tendons to tie the pieces of the frame together. Then they would stretch seal skin over the wood frame. It flexes side to side as well as front to back to accommodate for the waves. It's going to be awesome."

"That's what came in that kit? Seal skin and animal tendons?"

"No, it's all synthetic materials now, I'm just saying that's what they used originally. There's almost no one left who builds skin on frame boats anymore. Everyone prefers fiberglass kayaks, except for some diehard paddlers. I used to see bidarkas around Juneau sometimes, but mostly it's a lost art."

As soon as dinner is over, he heads back out to the shed.

When the first batch of smoked salmon is done an hour later, I've got the cook stove roaring, water boiling and all the canning equipment spread out on the counters. I've gathered all the lanterns in the house to have as much light as possible in the kitchen.

I bring the racks of salmon in, peel off a warm piece and smile as the smoky, sugary, peppery taste fills my mouth. I peel off a second strip and a third. It's like candy.

For three hours, I work until I've canned the first batch. With the cook stove roaring for that long, it gets warm enough in the kitchen to strip down to a t-shirt. In the end, I have a small mountain of food. It makes me feel solid, as if the road ahead were now paved. If we run out of everything else, we'll have salmon to eat and rain to drink.

I clean the racks and load them up with the next batch of brined strips. When I step outside into the dark fog, I breathe deep, filling my lungs with it, as the foghorn bellows behind me. I carry the racks one by one carefully out to the smokehouse, add more chips and get the fire going again as the light swings past. When I finish, rather than going back inside, I walk along the shore and try to figure out how to decrease the space that is growing rapidly between Kyle and me. *Maybe we should move back to town*, I think, *maybe to Mexico*, but I don't want to do either. I think about all the moving I have done in the past years, listen to the soft sound of the water under the fog and want to stay.

12.

WE BARELY speak when Kyle comes in for the night. I have just finished cleaning the kitchen while I wait to add more chips to the smokehouse fire to keep it going through the night. He mumbles goodnight and heads upstairs to bed. I wait until I know he's sleeping, climb the ladder quietly, pick up William Harris' logbook and walk back down the stairs. I light three candles on the windowsill next to the rocking chair, add a couple more pieces of wood to the fire, and skim through entries of north and south-bound boats, of storms rising and subsiding, until the following entry:

> December 23, 1977   0703   Getting harder and harder to be here. Never been so alone. Can't relax. It's so loud. Awful. Dark and windy. This is what I deserve, right?

> February 18, 1978   2050   Coast Guard food drop today. They came in and had coffee and I wanted to kick them out. They had older brothers or cousins who went to the war while they stayed home and did their math homework. The fat one asked if I'm a fag out here by myself with no girls. How can I explain staying out here? If I keep drawing, leave my gun in the shed, I'll be able to go home, be someone to look up to. I'll know when it's time to leave, just like I knew when it was time to come.

I stare into the fire. I want him to appear. I want him to be sitting at the kitchen table. I want to talk to someone who knew when it was time to come here and when it was time to go. I want to know if it helped him to be out here or if he ended up dead because of it.

Outside, the fog presses against the house, against my body. Everything holds perfectly still, the sound of the foghorn lingers between blasts. The smokehouse fire is almost out, only narrow tendrils of smoke rise from the bucket. I add overflowing handfuls of woodchips then close the door and wait, to make sure it catches. I pace in front of the smokehouse thinking of William Harris. I think of Kyle and me, the months ahead and a thick fear coats the back of my throat.

Once I see smoke seeping out the cracks of the smokehouse, I head back inside and settle in the chair by the fire, loud and popping now. I'll need to add one more batch of chips when we get up in the morning, then by lunch, the fish will be done. I stare at the logbook for a while before I pull it into my lap. I scan through the last of the entries of boats and weather until I find this:

April 1, 1979 2314 First trip to town since last October. Stayed a week. Missed the lighthouse, but not at first. The days are getting long and the wind is settling. I wrote to Sheila today explaining everything. There's no way I can send it.

I let the logbook fall back into my lap. April before he could leave again. Our nine month lease will be up in March, which means we may have left the island for the last time already. I run my finger across the loose edges of pages as I stare off into the distance which disturbs a scrap of paper caught between two pages, that I'd missed before.

William—
I'll drop Graham off on Saturday. The weather is supposed to hold. He's bringing two mitts. He's been looking forward to playing catch. He had another test and is

falling behind on his numbers. Can you work with him on it while he's out there? I'll be back to pick him up on Wednesday. Hannah

I stare into the night through the window. He had a kid out here? My heart lightens for him, that he wasn't so alone. He had a family that was giving him the space to take care of himself, to return to them.

I get up, climb up on the counter and pull the box of his things off the top shelf, make sure I didn't miss a letter to someone named Sheila. I put the box back then look through all the cupboards, find only the pots and pans and food I know is in each. In the curtained off area, I poke through the rows of cleaners, behind the paint cans. I notice the empty space, but it takes me a minute to realize the scraps of William Harris' t-shirt are missing.

The next morning I wake up before the light turns off. I watch the room as daylight begins to mix with night, Kyle's body wrapped tight to mine. I move his arm slowly then slip out from under his leg. Downstairs I build up the fire from the coals that are still barely burning and make coffee. Through the window I see that the fog has lifted, and that the smokehouse still has smoke seeping out the top. I grab a coat and check the fire, adding more woodchips to keep it going for another few hours. I cross the short distance to the greenhouse through the calm morning as it shakes loose the rest of the dark night.

I toss a few more bricks of charcoal into the woodstove. We decided if we keep the fire low, there is a smaller chance of melting the plastic around the stove pipe. Besides, neither of us is sure exactly how warm the plants need to be to keep growing. I check the broccoli and spinach and basil, carry each out to the cistern to water them. When I'm done, I close the door tight by wedging a big rock in front of it when I leave.

In the room with the light, I settle on the wooden platform with William's sketchpad. I have finished what I have come to call pane number one in front of the desk and have moved onto pane number two. William skipped number two or tore it out. I have to agree that it's not the most dramatic of the views, but I like the slow curve of the channel as it heads north and much of the sketch will be water, which I decide should be easier. There are enough blank pages to sketch the view through each of the eight windows. There are two more windows before I get to Knight Peak.

I sit and sketch for hours. By noon, pane number two is recognizable on the sketchpad in my lap. I tentatively shade and then erase because it's not right and then try again. Kyle crossing the island back toward the house from the shed catches my eye. I meet him downstairs, but instead of lunch I coax him upstairs to bed. I need to feel close to him if not emotionally, than physically. In this time at the lighthouse, our love making has changed from something of summer to something of fall. A certain cooling, a new crispness.

As we lie tangled, and Kyle drifts toward sleep, I fight against the loneliness that gathers in my chest. I suddenly don't want him to sleep. "I found out more about William Harris last night."

"Oh?" says Kyle, less asleep than I had thought.

"I found a letter. Turns out he had a kid with him out here."

"A kid?" Kyle rolls over to face me, props up on one elbow. "What?"

"I found a letter addressed to William from someone named Hannah. She said she was dropping off a kid named Graham and that he was bringing two mitts to play catch and she asked William to work on counting with him because he was bad at it."

Kyle sits up.

"I think it's great," I go on. "I'm glad he wasn't out here alone for all that time. That would be much harder."

"Are you fucking kidding me?" Kyle throws the covers and

pulls his clothes on roughly. He tosses things on the floor out of the way looking for his shirt. When he can't get his boot on because his sock is wadded up inside, he throws the boot across the room. It hits the wall with a dull thud.

I sit up in bed. "What's wrong with you?"

"Nothing." He is standing next to the bed pressing two fingers into the bridge of his nose.

"Obviously that's not true."

When he turns, his face is distorted in anger. "What was a guy who had a kid doing out here in the first place? That's great they played catch, no one did that with me, but what the fuck is wrong with these guys? You have a kid, you stick around to raise him. You don't run off."

I watch him, unsure what to do. He flicks his eyes to the window. "What an asshole."

"Maybe both William and your dad had a good reason to not be where they should've been."

All of the frustration of the past few months seems to have gathered in Kyle's eyes. I see clearly the extent to which the lighthouse and the weather has whittled him down to a sharp point. "The only reason to leave your kid is selfishness," he says with more anger than I have ever seen in him.

He stays where he is and I get up slowly. There is not much of Kyle that I recognize in this exact moment, but I keep searching. When I reach him, he flinches under my touch and I think he will push me away but instead he drops his head and I feel the warmth of a tear run down my neck. I don't know how long we stand there, I only know that we end up back on the bed somehow, without words, our lovemaking different again this time, more of me loving more of him.

Later, as we lie close against each other, I turn the words over in my mind until I carefully ask, "Have you ever looked for your dad?"

He shifts, tightens, but does not let go of me. "Yes."

I hold still, hoping he'll go on. "I don't really want to talk about it," he says.

I watch the way the dull light of the afternoon filters in through the windows.

"He took off before I was born," Kyle says slowly. "We got a postcard from him when I was five, and then never heard from him again."

"What did the postcard say?"

"That he was coming home."

And because Kyle's arms are still around me, I ask, "Do you know anything about him?"

"No. My mom refused to talk about him aside from saying she never expected him to be the type that would leave. They were married, had both wanted kids. I found a picture of him once. We moved when I was ten and Mom cleaned out everything. I found it where it had fallen behind a desk. Mom had thrown every other picture of him away years earlier. I'd never seen a picture of him before, but I recognized my own eyes and hair and smile. I kept it. I don't think she ever knew. In the picture he was jumping off a cliff overhang that I recognized from a lake not far from the house that we used to go to in the summers. There were big cliffs and small cliffs to jump off of, and he was on the biggest one. I'd only ever seen people climb up there and look over, I'd never heard of anyone actually jumping. In the picture, one of his feet had already left the ground and the other was pushing off, he was looking at whoever was taking the picture and he didn't look scared at all, he looked like he was sure he could fly." Kyle stops, his tired, broken voice close to my ear.

"From that picture I made up a whole day that we'd spent together from the bologna sandwiches to both of us jumping off the highest cliff, afraid of nothing. I went through the day in my mind so often that it got hard to believe it hadn't happened. Sad, right?" Kyle adds.

"Do you have any idea why he left?"

Kyle shifts. "I always wanted to ask him." He rolls over onto his stomach and turns his head away.

That afternoon, I can the second batch of salmon, make another batch of brine and prepare the last of the fish from the coolers for soaking. Kyle works in the shed, I can hear the saw distantly as I work in the kitchen losing myself in the task of storing food for winter. When I finish, I head upstairs, and pick up the sketchpad. The soft light of the evening is hazy and thick, lying on the water and filling up the channel. Because my back is sore from the morning of sketching while sitting on the floor, I drag the desk over in front of pane number two.

As I am positioning the desk just right, to keep the same part of the channel in view, I notice a narrow drawer under the desk. *Of course,* I think, *this is where he would write a letter to Sheila.*

There is a single sheet torn from the sketchbook, folded in half inside the drawer and nothing else.

There are two columns. Down the left hand side of the page is a list that reads:

Female, 608 lbs, Kenbel Creek, Kodiak Island

Female, 552 lbs, Salt Chuck, Kodiak Island

Male, 1279 lbs, SW of Annabel Peak, Kodiak Island

Male, 1070 lbs, Pork Creek, Kodiak Island

Female, 575 lbs, on the beach, NE of the mouth of the Gold River, Kodiak Island

This list continues halfway down the left hand side of the page.

"Oh my god." I imagine the bears. The list is too long to be killing for meat. My image of him healing himself out here is replaced with an image of a sick person who kills bears for sport or as some sort of sick vendetta, and I do not want it to be so. On the right hand side of the page is a longer, separate list:

> The man in the tunnel with the rats
> The man with the scar
> The man with the baseball bat
> The two men together
> The man who hissed like a snake
> The man who got me in the shoulder

This list of men continues almost to the bottom of the page. I count them, knowing before I finish, there are twenty-nine.

Suddenly, there is no air in the room. I have to be outside. I run the stairs, step out into the night. The light rain feels good on my hot skin. I want to be on the farthest exposed rock in the tail of the island. As far away as possible. I cross the island in front of the shed, moving quickly. That's when I notice that the saw has fallen silent, and Kyle is sitting on the floor against the far wall. The workbench is in the way of a clear view, I can see his legs only, which are not moving. As I start to sprint to the shed I cannot get it out of my head that he has cut himself, bled to death while I was not paying attention. The door slams against the wall as I push it out of my way, breathing hard.

Kyle is slumped in the corner, his legs askew, his hands resting on the shotgun across his lap.

Our eyes meet and it is as though I have never seen him before. "What are you doing?" I whisper the words. He doesn't move.

"It's loaded," his voice is slow, each word given space and time.

I freeze, my brain refusing the scene I am watching unfold. Kyle's hand rests over the initials WH that are carved neatly into the wood of the gun.

"Do you think he was planning on killing himself?" Kyle asks slowly. "That fits with him just disappearing, right? That's what my mom used to say about my dad also, that he just disappeared into thin air. Maybe that's just the nice way of saying a man realizes he's worthless and takes care of it himself. Maybe old William Harris here, chickened out with the gun, just got in his skiff and pulled the plug. What was he doing out here, anyway?" Kyle turns toward me, his eyes distant. "What are we doing out here?"

I swallow hard, the tight script of William's list of men flashing before me. "He was out here to heal himself. To forgive himself so that other people could."

"Some things are unforgivable," Kyle says, the anger returned to his voice. He gets up in one fluid motion, returns the gun to the dark corner where he must've found it and leaves.

I drop my head, his words ringing in my ears along with the slapping sound of a rope against ice and the sound of my own voice calling her name.

13.

FOR THE next week, the wind and rain fight everyday for the most attention. Kyle spends most of his time working on the kayak. At dinner each night, I watch him from the distance that has settled in again between us. I study his mood, look for the doorway, the thin part of the wall that the weight of my body might change.

One afternoon, I am sketching panel number three when his back against all that gray catches my eye. His hands are in his pockets, his feet at the edge of the sea again.

I lay down my pen, study the angle of his body to the rock underneath it. When I turn and stretch, I see the *Laura Ann*. They are just down the channel, heading our way. The radio crackles to life when I'm on the stairs. "Hibler Rock, this is the *Laura Ann*." I jog to the end of the island where Kyle is still standing with his hands in his pockets.

"The *Laura Ann* is in the channel, they're calling you on the radio." I am out of breath, already smiling in anticipation of Kyle's excitement.

He turns and peers down the channel at the approaching boat and shrugs. "I don't have anything to say."

All afternoon, I try to figure out what I can do to lift his mood and settle on heating water for a bath. Hours later, when the tub is full and steaming, I follow the path to the shed to tell him it's ready. He's bent over the skeleton frame of the kayak. The long ribs of yellow cedar that bend beautifully from bow to stern are in place, each secured to a series of perpendicular shorter ribs. I am struck by how fragile it looks, no piece of wood any wider than my wrist.

"Wow," I say at the progress he's made. The last time I was in the shed, he had all the pieces laid out in order on the floor.

He looks up, smiles self-consciously. I look closer. Every piece is tied to any other it crosses in a series of tight x's with a waxy thin twine. The strength is in the combination of weak pieces.

I follow his hands with my eyes through a series of x's, the middle part of each of his fingers are wrapped in duct tape so that he can pull the twine impossibly tight each time without cutting himself. I touch one intersection after another, each as tight and secure as the next.

"Where'd you start?"

The rain pounds against the side of the shed.

"The center rib." He lays his hand on the piece of wood that runs from bow to stern on what will be the top of the kayak. It's slightly thicker than the rest. "That's what everything connects to."

I look up at Kyle, imagine him to be my center rib, before I admit it's not true. Every part of me is tied tightly to that day on the glacier.

"I'll have to cut into it here." He makes a circular motion with his hand in the middle of the kayak, "for the cockpit."

The air in my lungs stalls, nothing in or out, as I see now, with certainty, he is not building a tandem kayak. As I realize with certainty, that if you hide most of yourself, there is not much for another to hold onto. I see that he is on his path and I am on mine, that we are not navigating anything together.

*   *   *   *

Even though it does not seem possible, the wind becomes more and more powerful as fall turns into winter. I watch the surface of the water erupt around us. I spend whole days inside sketching because it's almost impossible to be outside. After days and days of howling wind and blowing water, Kyle says, "I need to get out of here."

"Today?" The wind is a constant hand against the side of the house. The surface of the water is white and foamy and steep. "You won't make it."

"I'll make it."

Something hard and heavy lodges in my stomach. "You can't go out in this."

"It'll be fine." He stands up, walks to the door and pulls on his float coat.

"No." I stand to face Kyle. "This was part of the deal. We made a commitment to stay out here. You knew the weather was going to close in. Find a way to make it work."

"And tell me, Anna, why does it work so well for you? What are we doing out here, exactly?" His eyes are live wires, his face set in anger. "Don't answer that. At some point, I did want to know what you're running away from, but now, I don't." The wind sucks the air out of the room as he slams the door.

The cold rain gathers on my face and runs down my neck as I head for the beach after him. The wind reaches my skin through my thick wool sweater.

Kyle has waded into the water and is bailing the skiff with the old detergent bottle I cut open for that purpose. The skiff is heavy with rain and waves that have splashed over the side. The open water boils and rolls behind him. I watch his hand gripping the caprail, the smooth quick motion of his arm as he bails gallon after gallon of water out.

I stop at the water's edge, four feet from him. "Kyle!" I yell over the wind and blowing rain.

He does not look at me. The skiff bounces and swings in the waves. He uses his body to keep it from being tossed up onto the beach. He climbs in, and drops the motor into the water.

"Don't!" I wade into the water after him, frantic now, back on the ice and here at the same time. Everything I didn't say then, coming out of me now.

He stands wide-legged to keep from getting tossed out and pull starts the motor in quick successive motions. It roars to life between us and he points the bow out into the channel toward Juneau, choosing a six hour trip to the south instead of the three hours north to Neely on one of the worst weather days we've had yet. In that decision I see that he is not thinking at all, only acting, and am terrified at the idea of what his next poor decision will be.

I splash out of the water and run up the knoll so that I can see him better. As he pushes out into the heavy waves, he drops to his knees to keep his weight low. I watch him take one wave over the side and then another. The wind howls in the two trees behind me. He bails with one hand and keeps the skiff pointed away from the lighthouse with the other.

I follow his progress along the island until I run out of land. I stand at the edge and watch him get tossed so far to the left he has to throw his body against the starboard caprail to keep from flipping over.

I close my eyes so that I do not see him disappear behind four foot waves. The wind quickly displaces the sound of the fading outboard. When I open my eyes, the island feels huge and empty. My hands shake as I wipe sea spray from my face and peer down the channel. He's gone. Hidden behind waves, or underneath them, I don't know. I crumple onto my knees on the rocky shore and stare at nothing.

The wind swallows the sound of the outboard until he is fifty feet off the shore of the island, heading back toward the beach. I stand, watching him battle his way into the small cove.

After the outboard falls silent, he sits down on the bench and drops his head as the wind catches the skiff broadside and swings it on the buoy. He stays out there a long time.

I walk into the house, spend the afternoon in the room with the light watching the mountains and water, all of me used up.

Kyle spends the next day in the shed working on his kayak, barely speaking to me at meals. That afternoon, there is a break in the rain. He sets up two sawhorses in front of the shed. From the small desk in the room with the light, I watch him carve a rib of the kayak to exactly the right angle. His head is bent to the task, his body guiding the carving tool in long sweeping repetitive motions.

I finish panel number three and turn to a fresh sheet of paper in the sketchpad. I sit down in front of panel number four, in front of Knight Peak. I cannot make the first mark. I want to avert my eyes, I want to turn away from everything it contains.

I think of William Harris' list, and for the first time wonder if writing it all down helped him deal with it. I wonder if studying every inch of the glacier, recreating it now in this time and place will help me move past it. I want to tell William Harris, *me too, I am responsible too, there is blood in my past that I cannot wipe away.* I am still sitting there hours later when night begins to move in, the sheet of paper still blank, the pencil still gripped in my right hand. I watch the mountain fade into the night sky, the distance gather between me and it, again.

When the light flashes behind me, I see Kyle standing on the last rock of the tail, sea foaming beneath him, hands in his pockets, eyes locked on the far shore. I lean my head against the glass. I think about who might be passing in the channel, who might be using us as a point of direction.

14.

I SIT in front of Knight Peak the entire next day, the pencil gripped in my right hand, the sketchpad empty in front of me. By the time I allow myself to get up, late in the afternoon, I'm exhausted. Downstairs, the fire in the woodstove is out, the room is the same temperature as the concrete walls. I find the matches and some newspaper and get it started. I add a few logs and open the front door to see if Kyle's out in the shed. The loud whine of an outboard catches my attention. I see Kyle appear in the doorway of the shed and peer down the channel at the sound of the approaching skiff.

The halibut fisherman is heading up the channel. Kyle walks to the highest point on the island between the house and shed to watch him. I stay by the door. When he is just off the island, the man steps out of the wheelhouse this time, staring at Kyle. He is too far to see clearly and too far to yell to, but Kyle does anyway. "Get the fuck out of here!" He swings his arm wildly at the man as if to swat him away. The man doesn't move.

"What is your fucking problem you fucking creep?" He swings his arm again. I can feel the anger overflowing in Kyle and it makes me feel sick to my stomach. He was never like this before. The man doesn't move. Kyle starts in the direction of our skiff. I imagine him ramming full speed into the side of the guy's skiff with ours. He stops abruptly and walks quickly back to the shed. The man is still standing outside of the wheelhouse, watching us.

When Kyle reappears, he has the gun.

"Kyle!" I start to run.

He balances the gun against his shoulder and drops his eye to the sight. He pulls the trigger before I am halfway to the shed. The man in the boat disappears from sight. I do not stop running until I've reached Kyle. I grab the gun out of his hands which he lets me do. I know nothing about guns and so stand awkwardly with it, not sure how to unload the rest of the bullets if there are any others. I look back at the skiff. The current has pushed it sideways and there is still no sign of the man.

"I shot over his head." Kyle says. "To scare him."

"What is wrong with you?" I cannot take my eyes from the skiff. I am willing the man to stand up and show me he's not hurt. "This is madness."

The dual outboards roar to life behind me, the skiff digs into the water at full speed, spins and takes off down the channel. Kyle gives me a look to say see, he's fine, and turns back into the shed. I am left in the rain, breathing hard, gripping the gun to my chest.

At dinner there is a tight silence between us.

"I know you're upset about this afternoon," Kyle finally says. "But it's no big deal."

"I think it's a big deal to shoot at people," I say because I don't want to say what I know I should say which is *you are losing it, we need to go*.

Kyle shakes his head. "You've spent your time in Alaska in town, it's different out here on the water. Things get communicated in different ways out on the fishing grounds."

"You're telling me people communicate through guns?" I give him a flat stare. "This isn't the wild west. You're not Jesse James."

"And I'm not the first one to fire a warning shot at some dude that's too close."

"What if you'd hit him?"

"I didn't."

A small flickering light behind Kyle through one of the windows catches my eye. He notices me staring at it and follows my line of sight. It's not dark yet, but it's hazy enough that it's hard to see clearly across the channel. Kyle gets up, walks over to the window and I follow him. The man's skiff is at anchor again at the mouth of the salmon stream. He's got a small fire going on the beach.

"That's it. I'm going over there." Kyle says.

"No you're not."

He spins around to face me. "Don't tell me what to do."

"I'm telling you that's a stupid idea. What are you going to do? Shoot him in the chest this time?"

"I'm going to ask him what his fucking problem is."

"Leave it alone. He can camp wherever he wants to in the channel. We don't own it. He hasn't done us any harm."

"Yet."

"Right. Everything might've changed when you shot at him."

At that, Kyle pulls on his boots and raingear, leaving his dinner half finished. I stay at the window. I wait for him to climb into the skiff and cross the channel but he goes to the shed instead. After a few minutes I hear the saw start up and I clear the table.

The next morning, the heavy cloud layer is low and tight a couple hundred feet off the water. The wind has blown itself out. The water laps gently at the shore of the island, in soft conciliatory sounds that follow a fight. I see the halibut fisherman's skiff way down the channel toward Juneau. It looks like he's setting his gear again, but he's too far for me to see. Kyle sits up in bed behind me.

"Let's go to town," I say, "I think we could use the break."

Kyle rolls over in bed and peers at me where I stand at the window.

"It's Friday," I go on. "Let's stay the night and go out to the bar like normal people. And let's stay in the hotel."

"Who are you?" Kyle asks through the sleep that hasn't quite let go its hold on him. "You're saying you'd rather sleep in a hotel than camp in the rain?"

"Yes. We need a break."

"You don't have to say we, I know you mean me. But who cares, let's get out of here." He rolls out of bed and checks the window. "Let's go now before we lose the chance." He catches sight of the halibut fisherman and narrows his eyes. "See? I scared him out of this part of the channel."

We're tied up to the dock in town by 9am. The first thing we do is go to the diner and order bacon and sausage and eggs and fresh fruit. After we order, Kyle watches the harbor through the big picture window we are seated next to.

"You okay?" I ask.

Kyle turns to look at me. He is pale, thinner than when we left town almost five months ago.

I set my coffee down. "Living at the lighthouse isn't working for you, is it?"

He looks away.

I reach across and pick up his hand. "Want to go to Mexico with me?" We're sitting in the same booth where he asked me the same question a little more than a year before.

He half smiles, shakes his head no. And because I don't want to tease out if he means *no I don't want to go with you or no I want to finish what we've started*, I take it at face value, that we will stay at the lighthouse a little bit longer.

"There's D. Ray," Kyle says later that night at the bar, a huge smile on his face. He bangs Kyle on the back, buys me a beer. More of Kyle's friends show up.

My old boss, Linda, buys me a shot and does one herself. I hear Kyle laugh over by the pool tables and it makes me turn around. I realize it's been a long time since I've heard him laugh.

"Either of you going crazy out there?" Linda asks. Her face

is old and young at the same time and her hair is cut bluntly to her chin. She is the only woman in town that I've seen wear high heels.

"Not yet." I watch Kyle lean in for his next shot, tentacles of worry wrapping around my spine.

"Seriously," Linda says, "How is it? I could never live out there, and if Ben was with me, I'd probably kill him in the first two weeks." She pours us two more shots.

I push against the need to tell her that Kyle is slipping away despite the fact that there is nowhere to go. Instead, I think about the growing wood pile, the way the sea spreads out in two directions. "I like being out there—having a place, I mean. Suits me, for now."

"Shit. There's plenty of places in town you could call your own."

"You've worked here a long time, right?"

"Longer than you've been alive." She turns her head so that she's looking at me across the bar more out of one heavily mascaraed eye than the other. "Don't you dare ask how old I am next." She opens beers for both of us.

"Do you know anything about the guy who lived at the lighthouse in the late seventies? William Harris?"

Her eyes widen. "What a fine specimen that man was! Damn!" She slaps the side of her thin thigh where the tight jeans wrap the tightest.

"Did you know him well?"

"No. I slept with him." She shrugs. "Or maybe we didn't. He was still in love with some woman who kicked him out. Love," she shakes her head. "What a stupid thing."

"What happened to him?"

"No one knows. Never showed up in Neely again. He and Charles were friends."

"Charles? That comes in here?"

"Yeah, they were in Vietnam together. He was pretty messed up if I remember right."

"Messed up how?"

"Well, for starters, he lived out at the lighthouse. He was jittery. Nervous. Kind of a small guy, but handsome like I said. He'd always sit at the edge of the bar," she pointed to a certain seat at the bar and I tried to imagine that William Harris used to sit there. "Didn't like his back to be to the door. Go ask Charles about him."

I glance over at the seat at the bar that has belonged to Charles as long as I've known him.

Linda shakes her head, points into one of the dark corners. "He's started sitting over there. He thinks it makes him order fewer drinks. I think it's because he'd rather order from Tina than from me." Linda makes a face at the pretty young woman taking orders at the tables.

Charles stands up when he recognizes me. "Anna! Things have gone to shit since you left here." He is a little unstable on his feet, has a thick stubble on his face, and watery eyes, the same as always.

I smile as he squeezes my upper arm in a hello. "Good to see you Charles."

"Sit." He gestures to the chair across from his as he sits, wrapping his hand comfortably back around the glass of gin in front of him. "Tell me how the lighthouse is. Windy out there, huh?"

"Pretty windy," I agree, setting my beer down on his table. "You knew William Harris?"

Charles nods slowly. "We fought together in Vietnam. He came up here after the war, trying to get his head straight."

"What was wrong with him?"

"War used him up."

"What do you mean?" I hear Kyle behind me laughing again with his friends.

Charles leans forward, makes sure he has my attention before he starts talking. "Tunnel rats they called us. We'd drop in, run like hell as far in as we could, stab or shoot whoever was trying to stab or shoot us, drop an explosive and haul ass out. I didn't see the guy that day, but somehow Will did. It was dark and shadowy. The man had the most terrible scar like someone had scribbled down the middle of his face. In under two seconds, that guy had a knife plunged into my neck and Will shot him out from behind me. It was like a reflex, Will shot him in the dark, hit him in the temple, inches from my head. Will was good at it. That's what bothered him the most."

"So he went out to the lighthouse to sort through things?"

Charles nodded. "Will tried to go back to his life. He called me not long after we got back, told me about the gun in the glovebox and the knife he kept strapped to his calf. He knew it wasn't normal. A lot of guys were in the same situation when we all came home. Main problem was they missed the adrenaline rush of war. They missed that feeling of being either one hundred percent alive or one hundred percent dead, with nothing in between. I had a buddy who did the hiring for Fish and Game. I put him and Will in contact and Will got a job tracking down problem bears on Kodiak, back when they got the harebrained idea to raise cattle on the island.

"He was back in the hunt, kill or be killed. He felt better for awhile, thought that might clear his mind, but he realized eventually that he was just perpetuating the problem, and I don't think he really liked killing bears. They were just hungry, he said once. So he came back here, slept on my couch, tried to pull himself together. But he couldn't. He was drinking a lot in those days. More than me, even." Charles smiles across the table at me.

"That's a lot." I smile back at him and he nods his agreement.

"William took himself out to the lighthouse as a last ditch effort to get himself straightened out. I can see how what I'm telling you might cause you to get a bad impression of him, but he was a great man. You hear me?" He watches me closely across the table, his eyes narrowed and clear for once. "A great man who just got used up in that war."

"What happened to him?" I ask.

"I don't know. He showed up at my house here in Neely in the middle of the night after he'd been at the lighthouse for a couple years. He shook my hand, said he needed a fresh start. He'd been making kayaks out there, even sold a few and put some money away. He asked me not to come looking for him, he said he needed a clean break. I never heard from him again, don't know where he went and I never looked for him 'cause he asked me not to. That night, he looked the best I'd seen him look in years. I always figured the wind beat it all out of him out there at the lighthouse."

The next morning, the calm is still holding, but we both sense something is coming. There is a certain electricity in the air, a certain sliding toward something powerful. We don't talk about it, we both just pack up.

When the lighthouse comes into view, I am glad to see it, ready to be home. As I walk up the path, the same feeling I had the first time I walked this path repeats itself, but this time with more intensity. I understand on some cellular level now that this is a place where I might find peace. Hope seeps in for the first time since I dropped into that crevasse.

Kyle and I carry in the groceries we bought in town and then he disappears into the shed while I put them all away. He comes back before I'm done with a stricken look on his face. I freeze, dread filling me. "What's wrong?"

"He was here."

"Who?"

"The halibut fisherman. He stole my gun. And left a note."

"That says what?"

"It's time for you to leave the island."

I sit down at the table, a sour taste filling my mouth at the idea of someone having been on the island, walking around inside the shed and possibly the house. "How do you know it's him?"

"Who else could it be?" Kyle has started to pace.

"What does that mean, It's time for you to get off the island?" I know exactly what it means and I see the truth in it. The note was left in the shed, not in the house.

"It's obviously a threat."

"Or maybe just an observation."

Kyle stops pacing to glare at me for half a second and then continues. "We have to keep an eye out for him. We're going to take shifts up in the room with the light. We need to make sure we see him before he sees us. He's armed now."

"We're going to stay up all night watching for him?" My voice has cracked, Kyle senses the doubt leaking through.

"Fine, Anna. If you think this is some sort of joke, just say it. You don't go traipsing around somebody else's property stealing firearms unless you're looking for trouble. That's pretty bold."

I try to imagine some man on our island. Tying up his skiff on our beach, walking around our kitchen, maybe in the room with the light. "We need to see if anything else is gone."

Kyle nods his agreement. I race up the stairs, climb the ladder to the room with the light. I hear Kyle on the stairs behind me, hear him walking around the bedroom below. I go first to the sketchbook which is still open to the same blank page I'd been staring at for days. The desk is still lined up in front of Knight Peak. I walk the circumference of the room on the wooden platform. It bothers me the most to think of the halibut fisherman in this room, but it doesn't appear that he was here. It crosses my mind that he was not here at all, that Kyle made up the note. I shake my head to clear it of such doubt, alarmed that I would even think such a thing. I remind myself that Kyle is still Kyle. An uneasiness settles in, circling, until I have to run the stairs to get ahead of it.

15.

THAT FIRST night after we discover the gun is gone, I take a shift in the room with the light. I follow the beam of green as it runs over the surface of the water every ten seconds wondering what I am doing. We found nothing else disturbed or taken in the house or the shed. I climb in bed somewhere around midnight, my shift less than half over. Kyle takes over early. He stays up the rest of the night and the following night. The man does not return. All that happens is Kyle becomes sleep deprived which makes him even edgier.

Over the next several days, we walk tentatively around each other. The sea turns dark gray, remains unsettled. The rocky point of the island booms and hollers with each wave. The lighthouse begins to sing in the constant wind. Deep, hollow noises, quick refrains, constant chants.

Kyle's eyes begin to dart.

I like the motion of it all, the constant noise to drown out the silence of all the things not being said between Kyle and me.

"Tonight is the loudest it's ever been," he says as I add salt and pepper to the soup. He's sitting in one of the kitchen chairs, feet sprawling.

I listen to the wind scream outside.

He pushes the chair back. "I better go check on things." He means the light.

"Me too." I mean the wind.

The sound of his feet above me folds into the sounds of the house. I pull on boots and rain gear and step into the night. The rain beats sideways across the channel and piles against the house.

I take two steps forward and am pushed sideways for the third. I cannot see the ocean but I can feel it moving around me.

As the soft light of the house falls away, the landscape flashes before me every ten seconds in a flood of green. I pull my hood tighter and lean into the wind. With two hands, I push the rock in front of the outhouse door to secure it closed.

The plastic greenhouse walls snap in the wind. I wonder, again, if it will survive the year. Inside, I slide all the plants away from the wall toward the middle and add more charcoal to the woodstove.

I make my way back, rain running down my neck, having found its way into my hood. As I cross the highest point of the island, it catches my eye. The toss of a boat not under its own power. A quick green flash of too much hull. I squint into the dark rain. In the next flash of green I see the boat listing hard, its caprail close to the edge of water as the wind pushes it. My hands are suddenly cold.

In the next flash of green I see the hard shove of one man's shoulder and another man tumbling into the water. I race to the shed where we keep our floatcoats, grab mine off the peg next to the door. My feet pound the wet stones of the path as I run to the beach. The helicopter won't fly in this, but if the Coast Guard starts by boat from Juneau now, I calculate, they'll be here in three or four hours.

I throw the haulout line over my shoulder and use all my weight to pull. The water pulls back before it releases the skiff. There are several inches of water in the skiff as I climb in thinking only of that person in the water, only that I must get him out.

The Evinrude doesn't start on the first pull, or the second. I wipe at the water in my eyes, use my entire body to pull and it roars to life. I scoop water with the cut detergent bottle with one hand as I back off the beach and swing the skiff around.

The waves rise to meet me. As the bow of the skiff is pulled high overhead, I lean forward, chest level with the caprail to keep my weight low, but even then, I'm tossed violently with the skiff so that I have to work to stay in it.

Smaller waves on top of the larger swells splash against the caprail and spill over, soaking my legs and splashing into my face. I bail frantically, trying to stay ahead of all the water accumulating at my feet. As I head out into the darkness, my mind races, how will I even find the person? I need to get Kyle on the hand-held radio. He needs to know I'm out here.

Night presses in so that I cannot see farther than a couple feet past the bow. I am blindly climbing one wave after another unsure if I'm making any forward progress. I claw at the emergency drybag duct taped to the inside wall of the skiff. Because I don't want the bag loose and floating in the skiff with so much water, I peel only the top half of it free and then stop to bail the water that has accumulated in the meantime.

I have to bend forward to open the bag that is still half taped and I have to use both hands. Unbalanced, and with the tiller left to the will of the waves, I am thrown sideways and catch the side of the bench in my ribs. I breathe into the pain as I scramble back on my hands and knees and fish the radio free. I set it on the bench next to me as I use both hands to close the bag so that water doesn't ruin the rest of the contents. I may need them later.

The next wave catches me in the face. I cough and sputter, push myself back up onto the bench and reach for the tiller to straighten the skiff out. I've gotten sideways to the waves. As the skiff spins in response to the way I pull hard at the tiller, I reach for the radio and see that it has been swept overboard.

I check the light behind me, try to steady my hands as they begin to shake, and then head farther out into the channel.

I open up the throttle a bit more then back off immediately as the bow plows into the next wave and it breaks into the skiff. My heart beats hard against my chest, as I bail as fast as I can. I check the lighthouse over my shoulder again, to keep my bearings.

At the top of the next wave, just before the bow drops out beneath me into the trough, Kyle finds me. The dark lets go, replaced by an oval of constant white light. I tighten my grip on the throttle and toss over several scoops of water.

The spotlight skips ahead of me, seeking out anything that might be in the way. When I round the corner, the wind pushes harder against my chest bringing with it a thin sharp smell of smoke. The light carves a path over the surface of the water just ahead of me.

The explosion seems to happen inside my body as much as it happens somewhere deep inside the fishing boat. I jump, letting go of the tiller causing the skiff to veer sharply. In the bright red light, I dive for the tiller, some sound coming from my throat, deep at first and then shrill. The waves have turned orange, my hands have begun to shake. In glimpses between waves that are walls of water, I watch the flames climb over the fishing boat, crackling and roaring, running the length of the long arms of the wind. I cannot take my eyes from it.

The white oval disappears into all the red for a period of time. Kyle is stunned, caught, like me, in the beauty of something that should not be beautiful.

The light snaps back to the surface of the water, finds me first then begins combing the water, far ahead. I turn the skiff and lean on the throttle, following his direction.

The dark presses in as I climb one steep wave after another, gaining speed down the backside of each, my stomach left at the top of every one. The wind pushes hard against my body, against the skiff, so that I have to angle into it to stay on course. Ahead of me the spotlight moves in long searching lines. The water is past my ankles. I bail as fast as I can, one gallon after the next.

The night is an uneven surface stretching out forever in every direction. I wipe the rain and hair from my face and squint into the dark. In the trough between two waves I can see only water rising up on all sides. I am heading out into the middle of the channel, the boat still burning two hundred yards to the north.

Kyle has calculated wind and tide, is leading me in the most likely direction both would've carried the man. He is the eyes and I am the hands.

I follow until the light begins to move in horizontal lines, no longer stretching in front of me. In the way it bounces, I know Kyle is using the weight of his body to try to tilt the spotlight beyond its farthest reaches. I squint into the dark beyond. I can hardly make out the difference between black water and black sky. At the top of the next wave, the orange of a survival suit muted by the dark, catches my eye.

I wait in between walls of water, low in the trough, until I'm carried up to the top of the next wave where the full power of the wind hits me, and I find him again, well beyond the reaches of the spotlight, a man tucked into a survival suit, not moving.

I open up the throttle, head straight for him. As soon as I pass through the light of the spotlight, the night zips up tight around me. Everything is black, it's impossible to discern up from down, right from left. I turn around, focus on the white oval, which Kyle has not moved from the place where he saw me last.

A wave breaks over the caprail. I bail as fast as I can and readjust the angle of the skiff to the wave to keep a second from breaking over the side. Three would sink me for sure. Slowly, my eyes adjust to the dark.

I make my way in what I think is the right direction, then drop into neutral, afraid I will run over the man in the water. I scan the waves each time I am lifted out of a trough. Without forward momentum, the tossing is worse. Crouching low against the caprail to keep from going over, I continue to scan the dark rolling water, but I have lost him.

I turn, focus on the spotlight, which I have drifted far from. I can't tell if it's in the same spot, or if Kyle has begun to search for me, if I am where I saw the man last. I take another wave over the side and realize I need to turn around, I will not find him without the help of the spotlight. I reach for the tiller, drop into gear, and feel more than hear something scratch against the hull.

I scramble toward the opposite side of the boat and lean over. The man is just a few feet away, already being carried by the tide past me. I grab hold of the man's arm, then jump when his eyes open for a second before they flicker shut. "It's alright," I say over and over, gripping his arm with all my strength. "We're alright."

He is thick and cumbersome in the survival suit. I hook his arms over the side and pull hard at his chest. I wedge my foot and push against the side of the skiff as I lift up, my back straining. One arm slips and he slides back into the foaming sea, face down. The skiff has swung broadside to the waves and is tipping dangerously with each rise and fall. I kick at the tiller to spin back around the right direction while pulling hard on the man's arm that is closest to the skiff. I hook it back over the side and pin it there with my knee, breathing hard.

A wave breaks over his back and splashes against my chest, filling the boat. I press my foot tight against the man's arm to hold it in place and pull hard on the closest leg until it is almost over the caprail. Another wave knocks into me, pushes me off balance and the man slips back into the sea. The water in the boat, cold and still foamy, is half way up my shins. I leave the man where he is, face up this time, and bail as fast as I can with the detergent bottle and a cupped hand. Rain has soaked the top of my sweater under the floatcoat. I can feel the heavy wool against my chest as it heaves with every breath.

The man disappears as the waves rise between us. When the water level is down to my ankles, I throw the outboard into gear and climb the steep face of the closest wave. At the top, I spot the man again.

I point the skiff straight for him and when I get close enough, hook one of his arms over the side, wedge my foot against his wrist, wrestle his leg over, grab him somewhere in the middle and pull with all my weight. This time, the wave that hits us knocks him hard against me. I land on my back in the floor of the skiff. He lands on top of me, and the skiff rocks wildly. I scramble out from underneath him and wedge his body between two benches.

As I drop the outboard back into gear, his head rolls loosely from one side to the other. Another wave crashes against the skiff and splashes him in the face. I wait until I see his chest rise and then bail as fast as I can as we ride up the next wave and back down into the trough. Kyle is swinging the spotlight frantically across the surface of the water, looking for me. As I turn the skiff back toward home, the Evinrude dies.

The sound of wind against water fills my head, panic rising in my chest. I pull the cord, nothing happens. I wedge my feet and pull again. We take another wave over the side. The Evinrude turns over, sputters and then dies. I pull a third, fourth, fifth time as we are swept down the channel. A second wave crashes over the side of the skiff. There is so much water in the skiff, the man begins to float. I have to stop to bail.

I use both hands, moving so fast the muscles in my neck and shoulders ache until they go completely numb. I throw over ten, fifteen, twenty more gallons and then jump to the stern to try the Evinrude again. It catches on the sixth try. In the next flash of green, I see that we are closer to the mainland shore than we are to the lighthouse. I swing the skiff and head straight for what looks like a break in the rocks on shore.

I have begun to shiver. The man continues to float in all the water in the bottom of the boat. When we take another wave over the side, I have to let go of the tiller to bail again. The skiff has become heavy enough with water that the caprail is only inches above the level of the sloshing sea. My whole body shakes with the cold, and then there it is, a clear break in the rocks. I keep my eyes locked in that direction, so as not to lose which direction I need to head in between flashes of green when we are buried in dark water and dark night.

When the skiff hits bottom, I grab the bowline and leap over the side. The water is so cold it stings my legs. I tie off to the nearest tree and go back for the man, wrestle him over the side, which is only a matter of inches at this point. I drag him just beyond the water's edge. There is a thick barrier of trees on the shoreline, we need to be under them to get out of the wind and rain.

I drag and pull until we are under the lowest branches that angle from the trunk down to the beach, creating a cave of sorts. The man's eyes remain closed. I lay my head on his chest, make sure it is still rising and falling. The wind howls around us, but the rain beats against the thick needled branches of the tree instead of against our bodies. Kyle's spotlight remains hard and fast in the last place he saw me.

I climb out from under the tree, wade back into the water for the emergency drybag that is somehow still taped to the skiff. I set off the flare and Kyle answers by swinging the spotlight so that it is pointed in my direction and switching it off and on three times. I'm not sure if he'll understand the flare to mean I'm on the beach or if he'll understand it to mean help I am going down, to mean goodbye.

I carry the drybag under the trees, pull out dry socks and pants and a thin wool blanket. After changing quickly into dry clothes, I inspect the man. His face is all that is exposed, the survival suit seals off the rest of his body. I work the zipper to check that he's dry underneath. When I find that he is, I zip him back in, wrap myself in the wool blanket, keeping a layer between me and the wet outer layer of the man's survival suit and lie down pressed up against him in an effort to warm us both up.

After what feels like a half an hour, I set off a second flare from the exact same place on the beach, hoping Kyle will recognize that I am in the same place, which would not be the case if I were still in the skiff. He flashes the light three times in response.

I climb back under the tree and lay back down next to the man keeping my eyes on his chest, terrified that he will stop breathing. "It's okay," I keep saying, "It's going to be okay. They'll come get us. Kyle will have radioed. You're going to be fine." The minutes tick by as I wait for the Coast Guard. I try to calculate how long it's been, how much longer it might be. The green light sweeps past us every ten seconds. Kyle continues to hold the spotlight steady, continues to flash the light three times every so often so that I am not alone.

I rest my hand on the man's chest, keep talking softly to him, keep my eyes on the round oval of light. As the storm carries on around us, I watch Kyle keep watch over me, the cold sea between us.

The night deepens as the wind builds. I have lost all sense of time, do not detect the shift toward morning. The muscles of my legs begin to cement, my mind slows. I slip in and out of sleep or perhaps consciousness until I am pulled to the surface by the constant flickering of the spotlight against the black sky. I pull myself out from underneath the tree, and detect the deep rumble of an engine underneath the wind. On the horizon are the lights of the Coast Guard cutter. I set off the third of the four flares. Kyle blinks three times in return.

Back under the tree, I wrap the blanket tightly around the man, check his breathing again, and then return to the beach, count off one hundred jumping jacks to get the blood back in my legs. I pace the short distance between rocks, check on the man several times while the cutter makes its way up the channel. Eventually, the loud wail of a powerful outboard rises above the rain and the quick burst of voices on top of that. I light my final flare, hear them alter their direction toward me and then they are on the beach, loading the man onto a stretcher, giving him oxygen, wrapping me in a thick warm blanket.

Two of them work to bail the accumulated water out of my skiff while another shouts instructions. One of the Coast Guard skiffs will tow my skiff back to the lighthouse while the other transports the man to the cutter. The Coast Guard men work fast, fighting the weather. The last I see of the man in the survival suit is two medics bent over him as the skiff disappears into the darkness.

One of the men guides me into the Coast Guard skiff, which is three times the size of mine and handles the waves much better.

Kyle is on the beach when we pull up to the lighthouse. He reaches for me as soon as the skiff bumps up on the beach. "I thought that was it," he whispers into my ear. He pulls back to look at my face, kisses my cheek and pulls me to him again.

As the Coast Guard men busy themselves getting our skiff tied off and back out to the buoy, Kyle and I make our way back up to the house. At the top of the path I reach for him and he pulls me tight against him again. In the chaos of the night, against his warm chest, I cry for the first time since before the glacier trip. The night has pulled everything else from me so that the only thing that remains are the most packed away parts, finally exposed to the wind and the rain.

He urges me slowly toward the house. He has the wood stove loaded with wood, burning hot. He settles me in the rocking chair still wrapped in the blanket and crouches next to me, studying my face.

"I'm okay," I say.

He squeezes in next to me in the rocking chair, his arms tight around my body. I am done crying, in its place, a wide, flat calm.

"Why weren't you on the radio?" he asks.

"I lost it."

"You knew the skiff was too small for those waves," he says.

"I had to go."

There is a knock at the door and then one of the Coast Guard men steps in. His head is bare, rain drips off his short hair. He looks to be about the same age as us. He seems embarrassed when he sees that we are both in the rocking chair together. Kyle moves me gently, stands up.

"Captain got wind of the detergent bottle. He wants me to

leave an automatic bailer with you. I'll just put it in the shed?" He turns toward the door.

"Thanks." Kyle says. When the door closes, he busies himself making me tea, adding more wood to the fire. I watch him from a far off place, wrapped in a new calm.

When the man comes back in, he's smiling widely. "Saw you're building a bidarka. What a cool boat, man." His eyes are animated. "A guy in Juneau is building one for me right now, says I'll have it by Christmas. No way could I build something like that, it would come out all crooked. That one out there looks tight."

When Kyle doesn't say anything, only nods, the Coast Guard guy switches back into his Coast Guard role. "Captain says one or both of you needs to come in to the station to give a statement. Standard procedure when a boat goes down."

"The Neely station?" Kyle asks.

"Juneau."

"I'll get our things together," Kyle says, already turning toward the stairs.

I look up at him. "You go. I'll stay." Whatever change has started in me needs space and time. I do not want to interrupt it.

"What? Come on. You're not staying out here by yourself."

"I am. Going to stay out here by myself." I add. I make myself say the words to make sure I mean them.

From the doorway, the Coast Guard man says, "Next patrol will be in about two weeks. We can drop you off again, then." He turns and walks out the front door, pulling it closed behind him.

Kyle's eyes shift back to mine. "You can't stay out here alone."

"I can."

"Anna, there's some creepy dude with a gun lurking around."

"He hasn't come back. I get the feeling he doesn't mean any harm anyway."

Kyle stares at me. "This is crazy. We're going to Juneau together."

"No. You need to leave, you need a break, and I need to stay."

"Why do you need to stay?"

"I just do."

A look of annoyance crosses his face, displacing the concern that had been there. There are voices down on the beach as the Coast Guard men gather back at the skiff, ready to go.

"You need the break," I say. "Take it."

He runs the stairs two at a time, throws things into a duffle which he reappears with slung over his shoulder.

I stand on the rocky beach watching the wake of the skiff until it slips into the night, my stomach tightening.

As I start back up the path, I wrap my arms tight around my shoulders, walk faster, suddenly wanting walls on all sides of me.

In the kitchen, I stand and look around. The room is too big. I climb the stairs to the second floor, then the ladder into the room with the light. The blind makes its slow constant movement and the wind pushes at the glass in great bursts. I curl into a corner where the wooden platform tucks up against two panes of glass.

With the heat from the light and the rising heat from the woodstove it's warm in the room. The glass against my side is cold. The two temperatures equalize somewhere in my body. I am afraid to be here alone, but some part of me knows this is what it will take. The sea beneath me, dark and full of motion, rises to meet the sea within me.

16.

THE NEXT day, I walk the perimeter of the island, exploring the boundaries, the exact space I can expand into during this time on my own.

At the north end, I climb onto the rocks exposed by the low tide, which is where I find the first piece of the boat. It's not much. Only a two foot section of wood, charred and black. The sea giving back what it has taken. An apology under pale blue skies. I leave it bouncing between rocks.

I climb the stairs to the room with the light, and sit down in front of Knight Peak. I do not feel as calm or as brave as I did the night before. I close my eyes, try to trust that it's still in me somewhere, that I can get back to it. I stare at the blank page in front of me and then at the upper edge of glacier, notice again the way ice rubs against rock. I roll the pencil between my fingers and make the first short, sharp line.

And with that, it all comes rushing back in. I try a second line, the far edge of the peak and my hand begins to shake. I am back in the belly of the glacier, everything is blue and white and cold and below me, black. *Can you hear me?* The ice rejects my voice, throws it back at me, a hollow, fearful sound.

I close my eyes and yell her name again. There is no answer. Far below I can see a small narrow ice shelf, three feet by ten feet hanging over the black hole that the crevasse funnels into.

Above me, the sky narrows to a thin slice of gray. The air feels stale, caught between walls of ice. Hard, sharp pieces break off under my crampons as I walk my feet down the wall while lowering myself with the rope.

Before I stand on the shelf, I hang above it, search for any sign that it might've broken Elizabeth's fall. She would've hit it after falling one hundred feet, would most likely be bleeding somewhere deep inside her body.

I raise my eyes to the peak through the windows of the lighthouse, readjust my grip on the pencil and try again. I sketch in the closest side of the mountain until it hits the glacier.

The ice shelf was as rough as concrete, impossible to discern any one mark from any other. I lowered myself until I was standing on the shelf, the sheer walls of the crevasse pressing in. I scooted toward the edge and made myself peer over. My mind began to race, my breath coming fast. *How could this have happened?* If I'd been in my tent I could've talked her out of it. *I didn't mean right now, goddamn it, I didn't mean leave right now.* I closed my eyes, saw again her steady gait, told myself she could've made it, if anyone could make it back to town, it would be Elizabeth.

I opened my eyes and focused on the light of the opening far above me. I hung onto the rope with both hands, suddenly terrified at the idea of being in there without it as she would've been, with no one to hear a scream for help. Below me, the ice funneled into smooth walls, forming a ten foot wide chute that was so dark I couldn't see more than a foot into it.

"Elizabeth!" I yelled into the chute, more fear than question. I fought against the blinding desire to get out, to be on top instead of inside. I peered into the gaping hole again, tried to discern if it opened up, if the bottom was close, if she was down there, unconscious.

I lay on my stomach and dropped an arm in. "Elizabeth!"

It was only ice and cold, stale air. I got to my feet, and yanked the line. A quick reassurance that I was not alone. Jason yanked back. I held my breath, tried to steady my shaking hands, and stepped backwards off the shelf. The chute closed in around me immediately. I focused on breathing, was too afraid of the sound of my voice to use it.

I saw Elizabeth in my mind's eye, walking confidently across the glacier as she had every day for the past two weeks, under a huge pack. She would not have mis-stepped. I heard myself again, encouraging her into the world.

The cold air turned sharp as I lowered myself farther and farther into the darkness. The only sound was my breathing. The tunnel curved a bit so that I could no longer see the opening. It was too dark to see my hand in front of my face. I closed my eyes against the hard panic that was rising. I lowered myself another three feet, and then another, and felt the walls press in even tighter.

I made myself yell her name, the ice absorbing the sound as soon as it was uttered. There was no answer, only a dull roar, which I slowly realized was the sound of water rushing hard and fast somewhere not too far below me. I imagined her body, my body, falling into that secret river, carried deeper under the ice, into a chute like this one filled up with water, where there was no opening, no way out. I couldn't get a breath, there was not enough air. I had to get out.

In one quick motion, I pulled ice axes out of my backpack, swung both hard until each gripped the ice, kicked the toes of both crampons in and pulled and skidded up two or three feet. I pulled the left ax out of the ice, swung it so that it stuck a couple feet overhead, pulled out the right ax and did the same thing. One foot and then another, my breath still too fast, the air too thin and dark, the surface too far away.

It took Jason a minute to realize I'd changed directions. He pulled the slack out of the rope, until it was snug again. I kept moving, hand, hand, foot, foot, blind in the dark, still struggling for each breath. My lungs were being squeezed. Hand, hand, foot, foot, the sound of ice breaking under my axes filled up the tunnel. The muscles of my arms burned as I reached over and over, pulling myself up and up until I was lying on the shelf, panting, the dull light of the day filtering in through the crack far above.

I rested my face against the ice, breathing, still gripping both ice axes tightly. When I pushed up onto my elbows I saw the two small drops of blood. I thought they were from me at first, my nose, or maybe a scrape. But they were frozen into the ice. Captured earlier, and saved.

Everything left me at once. My voice, my ability to move, the future. I stayed there, on my elbows on the ice staring at the two drops of blood for so long Jason tugged the line, as if to say, *are you okay.*

No, I am not okay, this will never be okay.

I made myself stand, made myself swing an ax, leaving Elizabeth in the body of the glacier. I made myself swing the other, leaving myself along with her.

When I climbed over the edge, all the kids were gone. Jason studied my face, asked the question without words.

"Blood," I said, "there's blood. And the bottom is water. It empties into water."

We didn't talk anymore, we didn't touch. He stood still behind me for a while before he got on the phone to call off the search. I stayed where I was on the ice at the edge of the crevasse. I felt the cold dark of the tunnel closing in around me again, constricting my chest, freezing my outside layers solid.

Jason pulled the gear and coiled ropes behind me. He set up his tent. We didn't have any food. "Come on," he said, "you need to warm up. The helicopter can't come get us for awhile. They've got a couple guys searching the other crevasse."

She wasn't in the other crevasse. It wasn't deep, they walked around on the bottom.

That afternoon, two Search and Rescue men set up their own ropes in the same place Jason and I had earlier in the day. They would double check this one as well, just to make sure. The man disappeared from sight within seconds. We all followed his progress by the rhythmic snapping of the rope against the ice as he went deeper and deeper into the glacier.

Finally, the rope fell still. I held my breath. I imagined him unafraid of the tunnel, able to go farther down, maybe there was another shelf I was too afraid to get to. I imagined him collecting Elizabeth, her long hair falling over his shoulder.

The rope began to move.

I shut my eyes.

He emerged alone.

"I followed it until I hit water." He shook his head, one short, quick, finished movement.

They began coiling ropes and slowly making their way back to the helicopter. Someone picked up my pack. I could not make myself move from the edge of the crevasse. I heard footsteps, felt an arm around my shoulder. "I'm going to stay here," I said.

The Search and Rescue man who had gone into the crevasse knelt beside me. "You can't. You're already hypothermic."

"She can't be gone." I looked up into his face.

"She's gone."

"It's my fault." His face didn't change, but his eyes did. He gently pulled me to my feet and led me to the waiting helicopter.

Elizabeth's parents arrived in town within two hours of us. I sat, shivering, across from them in the cramped office of the guiding service. Brad sat next to me, shifting in his seat. Elizabeth's backpack leaned up against one wall. Her mother was thin, with the same cheekbones and long dark hair.

Elizabeth's father had on a sport coat. He'd sent the helicopter back out in a rage. Had demanded different men with different ropes. Brad conceded, called Juneau, convinced them to come back.

"There's an extra seat in the helicopter. Do you want to go?" he asked Elizabeth's father.

"You're damn right, I'm going," he said as he stood, slamming the door to the office behind him. Brad followed him out of the room, leaving me with Elizabeth's mom.

She sat, back straight, hands in her lap, no muscles moving, and stared at me, cataloguing forever, it seemed, the curve of my lip, the turn of my nose.

"How is it," she said in carefully measured words, "that you get married and have a baby and you do everything that you are able to do to make it all right then you end up here?" She stared into my eyes. "What am I supposed to do from here?" As soon as her face began to convey any emotion at all, she regained control of it.

She pushed a stray piece of bangs out of her eyes. "She called me mousy before she left. Thing is, she's right. Her father thought this was the perfect punishment for what she pulled at our anniversary. The last straw, he called it. It's cold, she hates cold. I agreed because I thought it might show her her own strength. I thought that this trip might help her choose a different life than I did." The smooth surface of her face broke and she covered it with her hands as she cried.

I needed to tell her that I was sorry, that it was my fault. I wanted to tell her every single thing Elizabeth had said in the weeks that I'd known her, every kind thing she did, that what she thought might happen to her daughter did happen. Instead, I sat silent, caving in on myself, until most of me was buried.

I stare at Knight Peak from the top of the lighthouse. It stands as it did that day, unchanged, despite all that has changed.

I look at what I have sketched, two sides of one peak, I try to add to it, but instead see Elizabeth's face, hear her father's voice, see Jason's face when I climbed out of the crevasse. I see Elizabeth walking sure-footed across the ice and I cannot be inside any longer. I have the same feeling I had in the dark chute, the water pulling me toward it. I had to get out.

That caged, unbearable feeling intensified when the second helicopter came back with the same news, when the police showed up, took Elizabeth's mom by the elbow, guided her away and then sat down across from me at the table and asked me four hours worth of questions, behind a closed door. Four hours of *What was your impression of Elizabeth's mental state? Where exactly did you take them? Were you clear about the dangers of the ice? Did you encourage solo exploring? Did Brad suggest that you encourage solo exploring of the glacier?*

In the end, they gave me back my ID and let me go. I walked past Jason who was slumped in a chair, next on the list for the cops. I avoided his eyes, walked out of the office with my driver's license and my credit card and kept going. It was all I could do not to run the road that led out of town. I had on boots, pants, a sweater and a jacket. I left my backpack and all my ice climbing gear, my last paycheck, any words I might've found to say to Jason or anything he might've said to me. I thought if I just kept moving, it would fall away behind me. I could get ahead of it, not be crushed by it.

Eventually, a woman in a beat up Subaru picked me up and asked if I would drive while she slept. I drove south all through the night and into the morning, only stopping when we had to for gas. She slept all the next day and I kept driving, keeping my eyes only on the road ahead.

Everywhere I look the wind rages, whips up the water and throws it around. I walk one lap around the island and then another and another. There is nowhere left to go. Eventually, I stop, sit down on the rocks. The channel seems to stretch forever in both directions, the mountains on either side severing any connection I ever had to other people.

I pull my knees in, try to block out the immensity of everything around me and within me. I am too small to survive such a big place. The light snaps on behind me. I think of William Harris, how haunted he was, how he chose this, how it helped, according to Charles. But what is this? He chose to come out here alone, I chose to come out here with Kyle. The light swings past me. No, I hadn't. I chose to come out here alone. I sit with this realization in the dark. I sit with it until the light swings past again, and I know it's true.

When night falls, I move from floor to floor, noticing every noise. I toss all night, dream fitfully about a fire on the beach, someone watching me from across the channel. I bolt out of bed and wake up when I am halfway across the room on my way to the window. I stare out into the pitch black, wait for the beam of green to swing past the salmon stream to show me I'm wrong.

The nightmares return, every detail of the crevasse relived. In the afternoons, I avoid the sketchbook and watch the ocean. At night, I pace. Anything to avoid the dark.

As I follow the contours of the eight walls in the upstairs bedroom, one slow step after the other, rain pounding against windows, I think about the man I pulled from the water, his chest rising and falling, and want to know that he's alright. I see him as I saw him last, tied to a backboard, being lifted into the Coast Guard skiff and try to imagine him walking around town, buying coffee, ordering soup and I hope all these things are true.

Every night is the same, I close my eyes and I am in the chute, calling her name. Some nights, I'm Elizabeth in there alone with no rope, falling falling until I hit cold moving water. I wake up gasping for air.

When the rain stops after several days, I walk the edge of the island and think back to that day I climbed from the bed of Kyle's truck to the front, that feeling I had of him solidly next to me. I stand at the edge of water, the night all around me, wondering how to get that back, if it's even possible.

I begin to spend long hours staring south, anticipating the cutter that will bring him home. I keep my eyes on the horizon, imagining him eating in restaurants, going out to bars. I tell myself this is a break that he needed. I imagine him coming home afterwards, snapping himself back into the puzzle of me.

Days go by and then a week. The serrated edge of loneliness rubs against me. I'm inside when I hear the distinct rumble of two outboards working in unison. I sit frozen at the table. If he doesn't see me, perhaps he'll keep going. Perhaps he'll set his halibut gear and not feel the need to come anywhere close to the island.

My mind flashes to an image of him walking through the door into the kitchen. I'm on my feet, having decided it would be best if he saw me, that maybe that will facilitate the same outcome as all the other visits. He will just stare and move on. He only came ashore when he thought we were gone.

The motors are much closer now, loud against the relatively calm day. As I reach for the doorknob I am gripped by the idea that he could somehow know I'm here alone. I let go of the doorknob. The skiff is close. I run to the window on the opposite side of the house and see a skiff that I've never seen before passing out in the channel on its way toward Juneau. I lean against the wall and try to calm my breathing.

One night, after tossing for hours, I wrap a sleeping bag around my shoulders and climb the stairs into the room with the light. Settling into the corner, I search the thick night that stretches before me. I cannot distinguish anything until the light flashes by, burning images of water and rock into my vision that persist once the night closes in again. I count ten seconds under my breath. Remember the dark of the chute, the way Jason had said, *At least it was quick.* It was the last time we spoke, before her parents arrived.

Climbing back into bed, Kyle's open duffle that serves as a dresser catches my eye. His watch is thrown on top. I buckle it onto my own wrist, and curl up on the bed.

The wind stacks up the water and throws it against the shore all day and all night. I begin to notice that when I sit at the table, I face south; when I lie in the bathtub, I face south.

I am battening down the walls of the greenhouse so that

they will not snap so violently in the wind when I see the Coast Guard cutter heading straight toward the island. The high white bow small on the horizon, a mile out at least, makes me feel like laughing.

I run into the house, but there is nothing to do in there. Down on the beach I pace, calculate time and distance, measure the progress of the boat until it is almost even with the island. I anticipate the slowing until I almost see it. I search the deck for Kyle's shape, but the boat is too far away. My eyes lock on the bow wave, the curl of water that will decrease when the boat slows.

It passes at full speed, giving me two long taps of the horn.

I sit down on the small rocks of the beach. The ocean seems to rise up, crowd around me. I try to make sense out of what's happening, but my mind will not move.

Rain beats against my jacket, running in small rivers on the surface of my pants. I don't know how long I sit there. When I finally stand, my muscles pull back, locked in place by the cold.

I cross the island slowly, unclear as to exactly where I'm headed until I am inside the shed. The skeleton of the kayak is balanced between two sawhorses. I run my hand along one smooth rib and see that Kyle stopped halfway through one of the x's. The nylon thread hangs long and loose. I pull it tight, follow his wrap across the top of one piece of wood, then behind the second. I pull the thread again, unable to make it lie as tight as his last wrap. The nylon digs into my skin. I look around, find the duct tape, wrap each of my fingers.

As I work, my mind loosens. I tell myself there is a reason he did not come back. Something has happened. I feel the urge to ask the Coast Guard, but do not want to broadcast my desperation over the marine radio for everyone to hear. But what could've happened except that he did not want to come back? The nylon x and my fingers blur with tears. What could've happened except that the wedge I put between us by never telling him the whole story has grown too wide to cross? I isolated myself and in the process, Kyle too. I yank on the thread sharply, rocking the kayak against the sawhorses.

My eyes lock on the single cockpit and my sorrow turns to rage. I'd been so consumed, so wrapped in the past, there was no room for Kyle, and as a result there was no room for me in the future he was building. I bring my hand down hard on the center rib, which bows slightly under the pressure then pops back, shaking the entire structure.

I grab the hammer lying on the workbench and swing it with two hands. A deep dull thud echoes as the hammer smashes into the wood. The kayak jumps on the sawhorses under the force. I swing again, crying hard, seeing clearly now the web I have spun for myself. I scream, a deep purge of all that cannot be said, the way Elizabeth wanted me to that day on the ice. It fills up the space of the shed. I swing again and the wood splinters like bone.

17.

AN HOUR later I am sitting on the floor of the shed among the splintered pieces of kayak. Night has gathered around me but I don't start the generator to run the light. I'm cold, but I barely notice. I am as numb as if I had been lying on ice. Somewhere deep in my mind I know I have to move into the house, that I have to start a fire and warm up, but I stay where I am. I don't remember sitting down but eventually realize I am half underneath the workbench next to a small trash can. I order my legs to move. My body is cold enough to make it clumsy. As I get to my feet, I kick over the trashcan. Several paper towels are kicked free, the stub of a pencil and a crumpled piece of thicker paper.

The paper has been folded so that it fits into the size of a fist and then crumpled from there. The folded creases are thick, it has been that way for a long time. I unfold it and am staring at half of a postcard with a picture of Hibler Rock on the front. The top half of the lighthouse is gone but the bottom half along with the island and all of the outbuildings stand unchanged. I flip the postcard over. In small neat script are the words: *I'm coming home to you. I'll be there as soon as*

The handwriting is William Harris'. My mind flails in an attempt to understand. Did he write this to Graham and not send it? The address is the part that is gone, along with the corner where the postmark would be if it had been sent. Did William Harris crumple it up and toss it in this trashcan twenty years ago? And then I realize this is the postcard Kyle's father sent to him. I dig through the rest of the trashcan looking for the other half that would contain the address, which is not in there. I search the floor thinking perhaps the other half was flung somewhere with the rest of the contents of the trash, but don't find it.

I am on my feet pacing, blood running again through my body. My mind takes advantage of this, forces me into the house where I build a fire. I resume pacing as I wait for the room to heat. *What are we doing out here?* The words pound in my brain. Kyle asked me not too long ago and now I need to ask him.

*   *   *   *   *

The beginning of December comes and goes over the next couple days, as I begin to track the weather closely. I study the small changes in the wind, don't miss a single marine weather forecast on the radio. I pack a bag, take notes, look for any patterns in the weather I had not noticed before, any small openings.

After three mornings of calm in a row, I wake up to a fourth. I wait for daylight, check the packed dry bag one last time, sling it over my shoulder, check that the fire is out in the woodstove and scramble down to the beach quickly before I can change my mind.

My whole body tightens as the surface slides and pushes under the skiff. I open up the throttle and cross the shortest side of the channel feeling over exposed, knowing the wind is only holding its breath, that the sea can promise me nothing. I tuck in next to the shoreline as close as I dare to the hidden rocks, and turn south.

After two hours, the wind is hard at my back. The skiff is tossed and thrown, I am bailing along with the automatic bailer to keep up with the amount of water splashing over the side. I have wedged both feet between the benches, am keeping my body low as my heart pounds in my chest. The farther south I go, the shoreline becomes rockier and steeper, offering nowhere to land. I can feel the anxiety like long ribbons pulling tight around my stomach and lungs.

The lighthouse has disappeared behind me, there is nothing

but open sea and wind and sheer cliffs and somewhere far ahead, Juneau.

The calm of the morning does not last as long as the previous mornings. The pattern I thought I could see dissolves now that I am out in it. I shake with the cold, know I've got to find somewhere to beach the skiff, that the wind will continue to build, that it's already almost too much. I try to point my mind in that direction but it refuses. Instead, it hovers somewhere above me, watching, waiting.

I can no longer feel my hand gripped tight on the tiller. I am twisting around, trying to figure out how to drive with the other hand when I spot a break in the rocks far on the other side of the channel.

I squint through the rain, not wanting to cross the steep waves and blowing water between me and the other side. It's not as bad as the night the boat sank, the difference is there is no oval of light, there is no Kyle. For the hundredth time, I search the close shoreline for any opening, any place the waves do not pound into something solid. I peer back across the channel. Through the blur of misty rain and low clouds, I see it again clearly: low branches, a break in the white foam of waves against rock.

I turn the skiff, open the throttle and hold my breath. The bow of the skiff launches off one wave and smacks down onto the next. I keep my head bent into the wind and rain, my eyes locked on the small beach far ahead. By the time I have pounded my way across, my whole body is shaking and the water is shin deep in the skiff. Spray and rain have leaked down into my collar and splashed up my sleeves and pant legs.

The beach is twenty feet wide, tucked between two rocks larger than cars, dark with rain. Small gray rocks crunch under my feet as I jump over the bow. I climb and slip up an embankment to reach the trunk of the closest tree, which is so big I have to walk the line around it.

I try to figure out the tide, if it is coming or going, how big or how small, how much line I should feed out or take in so that the skiff will be floating, rather than beached, tomorrow morning. I rest against the rough bark, try to make my mind move. Giving up, I feed out half the line. My hands go through the motions of tying a bowline but it doesn't look right when I finish, so I add several sloppy square knots. I haul the drybag up the embankment where there is a small palm of forest.

The shivering continues, originating from somewhere deep in my body as I pitch the tent on uneven ground and curl up between tree roots. Too exhausted to get inside the sleeping bag, I pull it over the top of me and fall asleep.

I wake in the evening, thrashing, fighting to climb the ice walls of the crevasse with my fingernails, slipping, slipping, farther into the black hole. There are small puddles inside the tent. The rainfly is in a wad at my feet. I push myself back out into the rain to set it up, dig out a granola bar and make myself eat it, change into dry clothes including two pairs of socks, sop up the puddles and zip myself properly into the sleeping bag. I lie still, waiting to warm up.

In an attempt to slow the shivering, I pull the sleeping bag tighter around me. I turn from my back to my side, adjusting my knees around the roots.

At the first hint of light, I watch the sides of the tent as they hang slack. At some point in the night, I have wrestled myself free of the sleeping bag. A vague memory of being hot comes back to me, but now I'm freezing. I zip myself back into the sleeping bag and rub at my arms and legs trying to warm up quickly before I climb out, afraid of wasting any of the calm before the wind picks up.

When I try to swallow, there is finely ground glass at the back of my throat. I push against the heaviness in my body as I climb out of the tent into the dull morning light. I pull on rain gear, drop the tent quickly and push everything back into the dry bag.

"Please, please, please," I say under my breath as I pick my way back down to the water. If the tide is out, I'll have to wait for it to come in, the skiff too heavy for me to move by myself with no water. Through the trees I catch glimpses, but not enough to tell how close or far the water is. When I get to the huge tree the skiff is tied off to, I balance against it and look out.

The clouds are higher today, the rain only a mist. The sunlight filtering through turns everything a light hazy orange. The water stretches out flat and calm and the skiff is sitting on small gray rocks twenty feet from the edge of it.

"Damn." I slide down the tree until I am sitting. I miscalculated the tide. From the looks of it, I'll have to wait two or three hours before the water will float the skiff. By then, the wind will be back up. I sit, staring at nothing, the heavy feeling pulling harder at my body, sweat beading on my forehead. I want to peel off my rain jacket but can't risk getting wet the only wool sweater I have. My long underwear begins to feel clammy against my skin as it soaks through with sweat. It's too much effort to take it off. Instead, I wedge the drybag against the tree and lie back against it. I listen to the rain hit the wide skunk cabbage leaves all around me until I fall asleep.

When I wake up, I'm shivering again. My chattering teeth feel like a jackhammer against my headache, and my throat has accumulated more glass. I dig in the drybag for dry clothes forgetting that I put them all on the night before. I check the tide, still far from the skiff. The surface of the water out in the channel is now torn, the wind gaining power as I watch. It comes to me that I may be trapped on this thumbprint of land, held by the wind. My head pounds as I review exactly how much food I have, how long I would last. All I want to do is sleep. I shift against the tree and the drybag trying to get comfortable, pull my knees up to keep the heat in.

I wake with a start to the sound of waves slapping against the hull of the skiff.

I am out in the channel before I have truly gauged either the wind or the water. I know I should go back to shore, tie up and wait for morning, but I can't make myself do it. I peer down the hazy channel toward Juneau, guessing I'm about half way there. The ache in my throat and head has now spread to my entire body. I want to go home. I spin the skiff around to the north and pound into the wind.

The next three hours are a blur of crouching low in the skiff to keep from going over, bailing, water sloshing, weather building, feverish swings from hot to cold.

I do not remember seeing the lighthouse on the horizon or tying off the skiff to the haulout or the walk back up to the house.

18.

I WAKE hot in a toss of covers, my legs tangle in clothes and sheet. There is pressure, a heat rising in my chest as dull light spills through the window. I curl up on top of the covers, my body overpowering the cold morning air.

When I wake again, it is because everything is on fire. My chest is hot to touch, my scalp is tingling with heat. I stumble to the window, rattle the latch and push until it swings open. I breathe deep the cold wet air, feel every raindrop as a pin prick on my flushed arm.

Downstairs I find water and the first aid kit. I pour what's left of the Tylenol into the bottle top, push the two tablets around with my finger and swallow one. When the other drops to the floor, I kneel, pat at the ground with my hand until I find it and place it carefully back into the bottle.

Sweat gathers on my forehead, I have to go outside to breathe. I walk the perimeter of the island, unbalanced. My arms and legs are full of sand, my head floats in fractured light, every color sharpened, every shadow erased.

I tumble back into sleep in the afternoon and wake to a dark room, to wet sheets and a dull ache deep in the canal of each ear. The quality of sleep does not leave room for dreams, it is as though I am suspended, separated from myself in sleep, my body demanding what it needs most. I ease down the stairs, take the last of the Tylenol and curl up on the kitchen floor.

The next day I begin to count hours. The buzzing in my ears starts out soft, a boat in the distance moving closer. I pull on a coat, walk outside to check the south horizon, expecting Kyle, before I realize the sound begins and ends with me.

I shake my head and feel the sloshing, the ocean inside me suddenly on the move.

As the pressure in my ears builds, so does the pain. I begin to hold my head as still as possible, do not move my eyes or breathe deeply.

I wake to the sound of tearing. A long strip of Velcro in my right ear that someone is slowly ripping apart. I fold my arms over my head. It is the loudest sound I've ever heard. It's too hard to breathe, to move, to cry.

There is blood on my pillow, matted in my hair. I am cold, frozen in a tight ball. My right side has filled in with a thick silence, through which I can hear only muffled sounds but the pressure in my ear is remarkably relieved.

I climb out of bed and the room tips sideways. Fear pounds at my chest as I crouch, hands flat on the floor, holding on. My stomach folds in half as the room slides slowly back into place. I do not want to move, do not want it to start again. I stay crouched, the muscles in my neck turning to stone.

When the motion in my body settles out into something like sea-sickness, I crawl back to the bed, one hand, then one knee, one hand, then the other knee. I huddle under the blankets, lie as still as possible afloat on an invisible sea, as the pressure begins to build again.

The next day, the tearing in my left ear begins. It's so loud, I drop to the floor, cry out with the pain. I press my forehead to cold wood, palms outstretched. When it is over, I am breathing heavily, exhausted.

I wake to a terrifying silence. I get out of bed slowly. The room feels loose, like it could slide into motion at any moment. I shuffle along the wall to the stairs, afraid to lose contact with what I know is solid.

I need food, the house has got to be warmer.

I find bread and canned salmon. The door of the woodstove makes a far away sound. I am moving in slow motion. I manage a small fire and a few bites of food before I have to lie down again.

The next time I wake it's because I'm falling hard and fast, the ice sharp as knives against my elbow and my back and my legs as I pick up speed. I reach out with both arms to try to slow down, the water is coming fast, I can hear it somewhere below me in the darkness. When I wake up, the room is pitch black and I am still falling, my knees tuck to my body anticipating the plunge into cold water that will carry me into the depths of the glacier. I scream, unsure if I am dreaming or awake until the light flashes green in the nearest window, leaving me breathless. I touch my leg, the bed, the pillow, tell myself I am not moving, even though I have the distinct feeling of recent motion, an unwinding.

When I roll onto my side, I am caught in the freefall of vertigo. I grab at the bed frame, terrified. I do not know where the floor is, where I am, where Kyle is. I pull my head under my arm, my legs tucked tight underneath me. The rest of the night, I stare at the corner of one window, breathe in and out slowly, still as stone.

At some point in the next several cycles of night and day, I begin to eat. One night, I build a big fire, which takes me over an hour. I sit close to the stove wrapped in my sleeping bag and cannot remember why Kyle is not here. My mind will not reach past what I have most recently done or what I need to do next.

I am sleeping, much of the day and all of the night. Falling and cold whether I am awake or asleep, the two states blurring. I sit for hours in the rocking chair and watch the sea build. A piling up, an announcement about to be made.

The silence pulls me in tight. I become aware of my fingers against concrete, the press of lung against ribs, the punch of heart against everything else.

I think about William starting over new, about how much of myself I have given over to ice. I try to imagine why Kyle did not come back, if he will be on the cutter the next time it passes. The rain falls straight and steady as I watch the gray days. I spend hours each afternoon tucked into a corner in the room with the light; body against glass, the sea below. I cannot get William Harris out of my mind. I imagine him tucked into the same corner and wonder what came next.

*   *   *   *

I begin to feel sounds. Wood dropped onto the pile I feel in my feet, my own voice I feel in my chest.

Days pass in a haze of forced eating, keeping the fire going, and forced sleeping. At some point, I start taking slow walks. I stand on the edge of the water, watch the waves break.

Wind is the first thing I hear clearly again.

I think its blood rushing through capillaries. I continue filling canisters for the first proper bath I've had since I tried to make it to Juneau. I listen, hand poised over the water spigot out at the cistern—the hose that brings water into the house had frozen the night before.

It stops suddenly, then starts again, that north wind that rips open valleys. I'm so happy to have heard it, I laugh.

Objects grow more still although I do not trust them. Every day starts in fear, a quick re-ordering of ceiling and floor in the first second my eyes open, as if the room had been spinning all night and only now, reluctantly, rights itself.

A knock at the door is the second thing I hear. I am sitting at the kitchen table.

"Who?" I yell, the rest of the words spinning out in my mind but not making it to my mouth as I stand up, grip the back of the chair, unsure what to do. I hear my voice from a very great distance.

There is a muffled sound from the other side of the door. A voice? Something shifted against something else? My eyes are fixed on the thick doorknob. Fear prickles the hair on my head.

He has come back. He's armed. I am alone.

There is another knock. There is no lock on the door.

I back up the stairs slowly, and then bolt up the ladder into the room with the light. A large skiff I've never seen before is tied up next to mine. He's gotten a new one, my mind tells me. My heart pounds against the back of my throat. I lean hard against the window but cannot see who is at the front door.

Footsteps are the third thing I hear.

I press my back to the glass, eyes on the narrow opening that leads up from the second floor.

A deep voice somewhere in the house calls out. My name? I try to get a better angle to see past the ladder. There are more muffled words I strain to hear. His face comes into view at the top of the ladder, words in his mouth. The features of his face fracture for a minute, loosen as rooms have recently been doing, rearrange themselves and then slide back. There is something familiar and something not familiar. I see my name on his lips again. He is asking if I am okay.

Yes, I nod, breathing again. He is the man I pulled from the water. I move toward him as relief replaces fear. I am thrilled to see that he is fine.

"Doug Shane," I hear from far away and I nod again. His face is pinched, his eyes searching.

"I had a fever," I say, not sure how loud it comes out. He has not moved from the top of the ladder. "My ears—I still can't hear well."

He searches my face for a minute longer, squints and then there are more words I cannot distinguish as he turns away. 'Juneau' I catch, and 'go.' He climbs down the ladder and down the stairs. I follow at a distance. When I stop next to the kitchen table, he stops midstride ahead of me and turns around. There is great concern on his face. "You need to see a doctor," he says loudly and slowly.

"I'm glad you're okay." My voice is one part words, two parts buzzing in my head.

"I came to tell you thanks." His eyes look tired, and so does the rest of him. The stooped shoulders, the deep creases in his forehead and at the corners of his eyes. "I can't imagine why you came out after me—"

"I had to."

He regards me for a moment. "There's blood on your ear. Let me take you to town so you can see the doctor."

I rub at my ear, turn away slightly.

"Are you here alone?" He asks.

I act like I don't hear him so I don't have to answer. I throw whatever I find into a duffle and walk with him down to the beach.

*   *   *   *

In his large skiff with two huge outboards, the trip is bumpy but not treacherous at all. Three hours later, Juneau screams at us, so that even I can hear it. Jets landing at the airport fly low over town, cars race along the highway and rain hisses against pavement. Doug ties up at the dock downtown and we walk up the street to the clinic.

There is too much to take in; it makes my head pound. I feel the noise through my feet and against my chest. I glance at every person we pass, looking for Kyle's familiar shape, the way he leans into the rain, one shoulder slightly more forward than the other.

19.

THE DOCTOR scribbles something on a prescription pad. He looks old and annoyed. "You should've called the Coast Guard. It's their job to come get you for a medical emergency." It is too bright in the small white room.

"It wasn't an emergency at first. And by the time I could think straight again, it was getting better."

He doesn't look up. He tears off what he has written, hands it to me as he strides out of the room. "You should've had this two weeks ago when this started. It'll take care of any infection that's left. Your ears have healed pretty well on their own so far. Should be back to normal in another week to ten days."

*   *   *   *

I follow Doug up cold metal stairs that lead to a thin white door above a liquor store. He has insisted I stay on his couch, after waiting with me for two hours in the doctor's office where I spent so much money, I agree to the couch to avoid paying for the hostel.

There are clothes flung everywhere, which he picks up haphazardly when we walk in. The kitchen counter is full of pizza boxes, industrial sized bolts and washers, crumpled up papers, unopened mail. The apartment is small, but cozy. I cannot hear the wind. There is carpet and a couch.

"It's not much," he says tossing an armload of clothes into the bedroom, the only other room off the main living space besides the kitchen and the bathroom. "We both spend most of the year out fishing. It only gets this bad when Sarah's out and I'm home alone."

"It's great," I say.

"We'll see what the weather does tomorrow," he says, "It may take a couple days to clear enough to run you back out to the lighthouse."

I sit down in the corner of the couch, exhausted, wondering if that's what I actually want. "I'm sure the Coast Guard can take me back out on their next patrol, whenever that is. You don't have to."

He straightens up, a dirty workshirt and several socks in his hand. "It's the least I can do." He catches my eye. "Really."

"I'm just glad to see you're okay, I never heard anything…"

"What do you mean? I thought Kyle—"

I am so worn down, there is nothing left to do but let things be the way they are. "He didn't come back."

That same look of concern he had earlier comes back into his face. "You've been out there since the fire by yourself?"

"Yeah."

"Lieutenant Lawrence, the captain of the cutter, said Kyle told him he was going to catch a ride back out with a friend."

"Did he say who?"

Doug sits down on the arm of the couch at the opposite end. "I don't know. I never actually talked to Kyle myself. He checked in with the Lieutenant about me while I was in the hospital, to make sure I was okay, but never came by."

I close my eyes for a minute. "He probably just went out on a winter king trip with someone and they'll drop him off." *Or he's halfway to Mexico*, I think. "He used to fish out of Juneau," I add, looking over at Doug. "What was wrong with you?"

He raises his eyebrows.

"That night," I clarify.

"Smoke inhalation. I was fine after a couple days."

"What happened?"

He takes a deep breath which makes his eyes sag even further. "Usually we don't bother with winter kings, the weather's so bad in the winter, but this year, Andrew didn't have a choice, he'd lost so much money. We were on our way back to Juneau with a full hold when the engine caught fire. I'm still not sure what started it. The whole engine room was full of black smoke. I could hardly see. The fire seemed to be originating from the back corner of the engine room. I remember hitting it with the extinguisher, but then I must've passed out. Kyle said he saw Andrew drop me over the side. He must've dragged me out of the engine room and then gone back in to try to put it out himself."

"There was no one else on the boat?"

Doug shakes his head, and then adds, "Andrew and I were friends since Kindergarten."

"Sorry."

He stands, turns away, clearly agitated. "No, it's okay." He tosses the clothes that he has balled into his fists into the bedroom. "You have a right to know how we all ended up out there. It's just a strange thing to be the one who survived."

He flips on the television as he continues picking things up, throwing them in the bedroom or in the trash. Because I don't know what to say, I stare at the TV, and eventually have to close my eyes because it moves so fast.

When I wake up, it's dark out, and Doug is gone. In a neat stack on the other end of the couch is a pillow and a blanket. I stand up, straighten out my back that has been curled into a corner of the couch, shut off the television, and swallow another pill the doctor prescribed.

In the silence, I notice a hollow whooshing sound deep in my ears. It's as though the wind has permeated my skin, is now blowing inside me. I spread out under the blanket. A false light filters in through the window and spreads out on the carpet. Each time the automatic door to the liquor store slides open and closed, I can feel it through the floor.

The next time I wake up its morning and Doug's bedroom door is closed. My head feels clearer and the noise in my ears has decreased. I creep over to the window. A deep fog has buried the city. I find my backpack, brush my teeth at the kitchen sink then close the door quietly behind me, make no noise on the stairs.

I order a bagel and coffee in the breakfast place around the corner. Taking off my coat makes me feel too exposed, so I leave it on. I watch other people in the coffee shop as I eat, overwhelmed by all the voices at once, the sounds of the kitchen, and the chairs shuffling. A toasted bagel is an indescribable delicacy along with a hot delicious cup of coffee that I didn't have to start a fire to make.

After breakfast, I head down to the Coast Guard dock. When I see that the cutter is tied up, I walk over to the office.

There is a young man behind the desk in a blue uniform, hair cut short. He looks to be barely out of high school. "Help you?" he asks, when I finally step inside. The office is much bigger, more brightly lit than the one in Neely, but still has the stifled feel of official government business.

"Is Lieutenant Lawrence here?" I ask.

"Who should I tell him is here to see him?"

"Anna Richards." When he continues to stare at me, I add, "From Hibler Rock."

"You're the one who went out after Doug Shane?"

"Yeah."

"Heard you were in a sixteen foot skiff."

I nod, wondering if he knows where Kyle is.

"Impressive," he says before he turns down the hallway. "It was bad that night."

I rock onto my toes and back onto my heels with barely any motion at all.

When he reappears, there is an older man with him. He is fit and his hair is just starting to gray. He reaches out for my hand. "Anna! So glad to meet you. Tom Lawrence."

I follow him into his office, where he walks around the desk and motions to a chair for me to sit in across from him. "What can I do for you?"

"I wonder if Kyle mentioned who he was going to catch a ride back out to the lighthouse with?" I sit uncomfortably on the edge of my chair, my ruined relationship on display.

"He went out for winter kings with the *Susan Marie*. They were going to drop him at the lighthouse on their way back to Juneau, but that should've been weeks ago. He didn't show up?"

"It's fine. I'm sure he just stayed for another couple trips out."

A worried look crosses his face. "How'd you get to town? You didn't make the trip in your skiff did you?"

"Doug Shane came out to say thanks. I got a ride back with him."

"That's it? Just thanks? He didn't bring you some black cod or a brand new outboard or something?" The wrinkles around his eyes deepen as he smiles widely. "I've known Sarah since she was a little girl following her dad around on the docks," he goes on. "Doug would've been blown half way down the channel by the time we got there if you hadn't gone after him. It would've been terrible to have to sit Sarah down and tell her that her husband wasn't coming home."

"Andrew was never found?" I ask.

"He most likely went down with the boat. Kyle kept a close eye on him from the time Doug went over and the explosion happened. He says he never saw Andrew again once he went back into the wheelhouse." He tilts his head. "I can make some phone calls, see if Kyle's still onboard the *Susan Marie* or if he moved on to another boat."

Because I have that feeling of dirty laundry out on the line, I say, "That's okay. I'll go check down on the docks. Can I ask you something?"

"Sure," he says.

"Did you know William Harris?"

He smiles. "No, I was in high school in California when he was out at the lighthouse. I've seen that drawing of his up in the municipal building, though. He was talented. I heard they found it on the kitchen table after he took off."

"Where'd he go?"

"The story is there was no word from him for quite some time and so the cutter went out to check. Both he and his skiff were gone. They didn't look for him. Back then, they figured if you wanted to, you could just disappear and no one really stood in your way. You must've seen his name in the logbooks?" The Lieutenant asks.

"We found some of his things."

There are two knocks and then the door opens. The man from the front desk says, "Sir. 10:00 maintenance is waiting to be checked off."

"I'll be right there."

"I should be going," I say.

"Well," he comes around the desk, takes my hand in his again as I stand up. "On behalf of the Coast Guard, I'd like to say thanks. You were under no obligation to go out after anyone, in fact, I'm pretty sure you were told not to when you signed your contract, but I'm glad that you did."

I walk back through the streets of Juneau barely noticing the houses or the cars, trying to get a sense of what has happened. Maybe he did get hired on a different boat for another couple winter king trips if the *Susan Marie* was done for the season. Our stipends weren't much, the extra money would be nice. Or maybe he took off for Mexico, or somewhere else new and exciting.

As I walk toward the docks, I stare at people, houses, bookstores, bars, a drug store. Something in my chest begins to vibrate, my body's answer to the chaos at its edges.

Down on the docks, I walk each arm of the dock searching for the *Susan Marie*. When I can't find it, I look for someone to ask. I pass three men that look old and grouchy. I stop in front of a younger man bent over something at the bow of a wooden boat. His back is to me, so I wait. He spins on his heel, heading down toward the wheelhouse, then jumps when he notices me.

"Hi," I say. "Sorry."

He's got on work pants that dirt has been ground into and a wool sweater that hangs heavy with rain against his body. He wipes his face with the inside of his arm and looks at me. I step a little closer and ask, "Do you know where the Susan Marie ties up?"

He squints into the fog and misty rain toward the far end of the dock. "Looks like they're out fishing."

"Do you know Kyle McAllin?"

"I remember that name. Fished on the *Tara J* couple years back, I think. Why?"

"I'm just wondering if he's out with them or if he's fishing with someone else."

"Does he owe you money? Child support or something? Or are you just pissed off at him?" I stare at him until he cracks a smile. "I'm pretty sure he's still out there with them," he adds. "I noticed somebody new working with them these past few weeks."

"Any idea when they'll be back?"

"Winter king trips aren't usually any longer than four or five days, sometimes shorter if the weather really sucks. I don't know when they left."

"Thanks."

"Sure thing," he says. "You want to meet up at the bar later?"

"No thanks," I say as I walk away.

"C'mon," he says.

I climb the steep hill until I am perched above town. The rain continues, a little more sideways now. I walk uphill instead of down, until the criss-cross streets of town give way to moss, skunk cabbage, spruce and hemlock. I walk for miles because I can, no boundaries in sight.

I follow the trail through dark red muskegs and old growth hemlock, branches lacing high over my head. I miss trees. I miss Kyle. I walk for hours, trying to rest under the canopy.

But it's not peaceful. All day there are people passing me,

people talking so loud their voices stay in my head until long after they are gone. A wild landscape pinned down at the edges.

*   *   *   *

Doug smiles when he opens the door to his apartment. "There you are," he says and steps aside so that I can come in. "Feeling any better?"

I bend to take off my boots. "The antibiotics seem to be making a difference." I stand up to face him in the small entryway.

A woman, long legs and wide shoulders, comes around the corner from the kitchen.

"This is Sarah," he says raising his arm. "She just got back today."

She fits herself against the side of his body and his arm falls into place. A gesture as smooth and worn as old wood. It makes me realize how foreign Kyle and I have become to each other in the past months. "It's really nice to meet you," she says. "I—um—I don't know what to say, really. It—would've been—well, I hate to even think how it would've been." Her lower lip trembles.

I nod into the silence, glance at Doug. Her hand rises to his chest, rests there as her eyes fill. "It wasn't me alone," I say, because I'm not sure what else to do. "Without Kyle manning the spotlight, I wouldn't have found him."

Sarah wipes at her eyes. "I heard. We didn't get to meet him." Doug's arm tightens around her.

When she turns toward the kitchen, Doug follows. "Dinner's almost ready. You'll join us?" He asks.

The table is set for three. I am crushed by the normalcy of placemats, of napkins folded under forks, of Doug's hand in Sarah's, the ease of cooking without fire, without splitting wood, without going to get the wood, without waiting for weather.

"I'm not feeling that well, actually."

Sarah turns, watches me closely for a minute. "Can I get you anything?"

"Maybe I'll just lie down."

"Sure," Doug says. "Our room will be quieter than the couch. Sarah and I are going to stay down on her dad's boat tonight."

I follow him into their room, which is clean like the rest of the house is now. He must've stayed home all day scrubbing and vacuuming. The bed looks luxurious with a down comforter and extra pillows.

When he leaves, I lie down on the bed fully clothed. I am not tired, only exhausted.

*   *   *   *

The next morning, I wake to the sound of cars, to people on the sidewalk below the window. I have been in the crevasse all night. When I hear a key in the lock and quiet voices in the living room, I dig around in my duffle, find a clean shirt and my toothbrush. Out the window is a sea of low, milky clouds.

"Hey," Sarah says when I step into the living room. They are seated at the table, a bag of bagels between them.

Doug smiles widely. "Coffee's ready. Fog's too thick to go anywhere today. Supposed to stick around for a while."

I join them at the table. He still does not look rested.

"Looks like you'll have to enjoy the great metropolis of Juneau for a bit longer," he adds.

"It's nice to have a little break, to tell you the truth," I say because its true but more because I do not want to say that I need the time to find Kyle, to find answers, to try to fix what has broken between us.

"Do you feel any better?" Sarah asks. She motions to the bagels. "Help yourself."

"I can hear a lot better this morning." I reach for a bagel, spread cream cheese. "Thanks for breakfast."

"Of course. We're fine staying on the boat for as long as you want to stay here." There are freckles across her cheeks and nose and her eyes seem to smile even when the rest of her face is not.

"Thanks," I say again.

Not used to talking, I listen to traffic, a man yelling off in the distance, the door to the liquor store opening. I watch Doug's chest out of the corner of my eye. The steady rising and falling.

Sarah treads straight through my awkwardness, filling in all the space with her ease. "What's it like living out at the lighthouse? I can't imagine."

"It's windy."

She laughs. "How's that cistern? Plasticy tasting water? That thing's been there for my whole life."

"It's amazing what you can get used to."

"Sponge baths?"

"We found a tub at the dump in Neely."

"You dragged a tub down the channel from Neely?!" She laughs again. "Seriously, do you like it out there?"

"I do."

Doug steps into the beat of silence that follows. "Anna, you should know Andrew was a good captain. He wasn't some shmuck. Anytime I wasn't fishing with Sarah and her dad, I'd go out with Andrew. I trusted him completely." Doug leans forward, forearms on the table, the broken pieces of him showing. Sarah turns toward him, drops two fingers into the crook of his elbow.

20.

FROM DOUG and Sarah's, I head down to the harbor, walk the part of the dock the sweater guy glanced at to make sure the *Susan Marie* has not come back. The only empty slip is the very last one. From there, I wander the streets for hours, encased in fog.

I return later in the day to sit on the bench that overlooks the docks. I locate the empty slip again and then watch men bundled in identical raingear rushing about in the cold rain, wondering if I would recognize the gait of Kyle's walk, the distance between steps.

Instead, I recognize Sarah aboard a massive steel, sharply painted boat. One of the larger tied up at the docks.

She waves as I approach. "Come on up. My dad would love to meet you."

I climb over the rail and follow her into the wheelhouse. It is large and perfectly in order. A man in a clean blue button down work shirt is sitting at the table, surrounded by mail in neat stacks, opened and unopened. "Dad, this is Anna," Sarah says as she pulls the door closed behind me, shutting the rain out and the cold.

He looks up. He has the deeply wrinkled skin of a life-long fisherman, and a trim white beard. His eyes are the same color green as Sarah's and just as kind. "It's awkward," he says, "when you want to hug someone you don't know."

Sarah laughs.

"We can skip that," I say, shrugging.

He smiles. "I have one question. How'd you get him in the boat? He's over six foot, and you're a lot smaller than that."

"Luck."

"Hellova deal. I'd buy you a drink, but you don't look old enough. I'd buy you a whole bar if I could, for saving my girl there from a world of hurt."

I glance around at the rest of the wheelhouse. "I've never been on such a nice boat."

"I'll show you around," Sarah says.

The crew quarters, engine room and deck are just as immaculate as the wheelhouse. Everything sings of efficiency.

We circle the deck and end up at the lifeboat where Sarah has wrenches and hardware spread out. "I'm replacing the lashes," she says. "The reason Doug ended up in the water instead of the lifeboat is that the lashes were rusted. Dad thinks Andrew couldn't get it to release, so his only choice was to put Doug in the water."

I nod. We both know a person can survive in a lifeboat for a matter of days, but once in the water, survival is cut to a matter of hours.

"Want a hand?" I ask.

"Sure."

While Sarah locates another wrench from somewhere below decks, I stare up the channel toward the lighthouse. Maybe Kyle's already there, dropped off by whoever he went fishing with, wondering where I am.

While Sarah and I work, she asks one question after another. Drags it out of me that Kyle did not come back to the lighthouse, that I don't know really know where he is, that we started out one way, and then become something else entirely.

"When Doug and I get all sideways, we try to just start with something small. Work our way toward the big stuff."

"The big stuff seems too big."

"Dad says the biggest waves are still just water."

After we finish replacing the lashes, I begin to feel I'm in the way and leave Sarah to the rest of her chores. I spend the afternoon wandering around aimlessly, glad to be without the boundaries of the island, trying to sort through what is big and what is small and if it's too late or if there will be the chance to start somewhere. I think of the postcard and am dazed at the idea that Kyle has kept as much from me as I have kept from him.

At dusk, when the boats that are coming in for the night will return, I am perched on the bench again in a cold light rain. The first three boats head for the opposite side of the dock. The fourth pulls into the *Sarah Marie's* slip. I watch the deckhands as they tie up the boat and scramble over and around the gear on deck. They are all dressed the same in rain gear and rubber boots, but I recognize Kyle immediately.

I fight against the urge to run the docks, instead, I sit and watch him finish the tasks of stowing gear and cleaning the deck. I am surprised to hear him laugh with the others, to see the quickness returned to his step. I understand that what needed to change has changed.

He walks up the dock toward the street with the two other deckhands. When they reach the top of the ramp, I stand up. He sees me right away.

"Anna." There is relief in his voice and then suddenly he stalls, unsure.

"What are you doing?" I ask. We have not touched. His eyes are dark, hard to read.

He looks away. "I'm fishing—for awhile—I—I meant to come back."

"You *meant* to?"

"I'm sorry. I just couldn't make myself go back. Each time captain asks if I want to stay for another king trip, I say yes."

Anger gathers in me like wind in the channel. "You were just going to leave me out there with no word? For how long?"

He pushes his hood off, water drips down the side of his jaw, which is set in a hard line. "I should've sent word, you're right. But you don't need me out there. Our relationship has never been based in needing each other, Anna. Aside from working together on the house, you've always kept to yourself."

His words wrap around me in exactly the same way the crevasse does in my dreams, until I am fighting to get free. "No. That's not true."

"It is true," he says. And it is, I know it is. The anger drains out of me. I feel lost, as if I had come home to find every room empty and bare.

"Kyle, why did we go to the lighthouse?"

He runs his hand across his forehead, looks away. The rain has found its way under my hood, is running cold and quick down my neck.

"Answer me. Why did we go to the lighthouse? I found a postcard." His body goes still and in that moment I understand that we do not know each other, have never known each other.

The wind off the water blows rain between us as we stand there, not speaking.

"I need to tell you why I went out to the lighthouse," I say. The words pile up inside me, I feel them gathering at the top of the slide, Kyle at the bottom. Without considering, I let them go, trust that he will catch them. This is the only thing left to do, the only way to change direction. "I led a glacier trip three years ago on the Juneau Ice Field."

I force the words out of me, slow at first and then in a torrent, every last one of them until we are drenched, until Kyle pulls me close, buries his face against my neck and I hold on. "Oh Anna," he says as he accepts the weight of my sadness, adds it to his own. We stand in the rain, on the edge of land, our arms laced tightly around each other, two weak pieces tied together for strength.

*   *   *   *

I am shivering with the cold and the telling. Kyle keeps his arm around me, guides us to a coffee shop across the street. We sit in a warm corner over steaming cups of coffee, our chairs pulled close together. He wraps his fingers in mine. "I don't think you're responsible, Anna. Sounds like she left of her own accord."

"That's what the police decided as well, but that's not what it feels like."

"And how does the lighthouse help with all this?"

"It's the first time I've stayed anywhere, committed to something. It's the end of the running away from it. I needed the space and time to think through it, to get to the other side of it somehow."

"You're not done being out there, are you?" Kyle asks.

"The lease is up in three months."

Kyle's eyes cloud over.

"I need to finish," I pick up his other hand. "I've done nothing but walk away from everything and everyone since I walked out of the guiding office that day. It has to stop."

Kyle lets go of both my hands, rests his elbows on his knees. "Do you want me to come back out with you?"

"Do you want to?"

"No, I really don't. But I will."

"Kyle?" I ask. "Is your dad William Harris?"

He meets my gaze, nods once and looks away as he begins to talk. "From the time I was five, I knew I was coming up here to Hibler Rock. It was the only place I ever knew of that he'd been. I wanted the reason he never came back to be heroic. He was killed saving someone, or something. My mom hated it when I talked like that, she always said he just left, there was nothing more to it. When I came up here, she almost lost her mind, she was so mad. She couldn't understand why I wanted to find him. I actually thought I'd find out something redeeming. Instead, I found out he had another family. I found out that he's an asshole, that's why he never came back." Anger has clouded his face. His jaw is set in a tight line again.

The tears return to my eyes, hot and stinging. "Charles said the war used him up. Maybe he wasn't thinking clearly, maybe there's still some reason—"

"Charles from the bar?" Kyle interrupts.

"Yeah, they fought together in Vietnam. You didn't know?"

Kyle shakes his head.

"William shot a man out from behind Charles just before the man was going to slit his throat."

Kyle is watching me closely. I wipe at the tears running down my face. "I'm just trying to say, maybe he wasn't all bad. Maybe he did bad things, but he wasn't a bad person."

Kyle shakes his head definitively. "He had another family, Anna. He replaced me, turned his back." Kyle takes a deep breath, sits up straight. "Can we talk about something else?"

I nod, study his face, recognizing everything that I have ever loved in him. "Are you done with us?" I ask quietly.

"No," he says. "Are you?"

"No."

"Are you going back out to the lighthouse?" he asks.

"I'll have to think about it. It was hard to be there alone," I say.

"I should've sent word with somebody that I was staying in town. I'm sorry. I got lost in all this. And it seemed like you wanted to be out there alone."

"I did."

"You don't have to be invincible, Anna." He reaches over, rests his hand just above my knee. "That must be exhausting."

The woman behind the counter flips the sign on the door from open to closed, begins counting the register. "We should go," I say. "Doug and Sarah are expecting me for dinner. Will you come?"

As we walk up the hill, I reach for Kyle's hand and he does not let go.

When Doug opens the door he smiles broadly at the two of us. "Kyle?" he asks.

"Good to finally meet you," Kyle says. "I stopped by the hospital, but there was a lot of family there, I didn't want to intrude."

Doug shakes Kyle's hand for a bit longer than he might normally, but we do not dwell on how we all know each other, instead Kyle and I are pulled into the ease between Sarah and Doug, the way words, actions, looks, roll between them, not catching on anything sharp.

"Who did you fish for out of Juneau?" Sarah asks Kyle as she refills all our wine glasses.

"Dave Swenson."

"Ohhh." Sarah makes a face. "Did he ever do the bucket thing?"

"What's that?" Kyle says. "I hate to even ask."

"He used to be known for sitting over a five gallon bucket at the breakfast table with his crew so he could take a dump *while* he was eating, to save time when the fish were in thick."

"Not surprising," Kyle says, laughing.

"That's disgusting," I add.

"Who are you talking about?" Doug asks, making it obvious he was not paying attention before.

Sarah turns to him with a smile, "Dave Swenson. His son is Patrick. You know, the gold panner."

Doug nods his recognition.

Kyle and Sarah continue to compare notes about other guys in the fishing fleet. Sarah knows all the other captains Kyle has fished for. Doug eats, watches Sarah, rests a hand on her knee or her shoulder.

When the dishes are cleared, we all continue to sit at the table, chatting, mostly laughing at the stories Sarah tells of various fisherman. She is an only child, grew up out on the fishing grounds. The first time she has ever lived on land is in this house with Doug.

"So, how much longer will you be at the lighthouse? Or are you there for good?" She asks.

Kyle looks at me. "We're not sure."

"I don't think I'd last a week," Sarah says. She looks at Doug. "You might make it two weeks."

"Seems like it might be peaceful to be out there," Doug says.

"It is peaceful," Kyle agrees, "but in a way that makes you edgy."

I think about the view from the room with the light, the sharp loneliness of being out there alone. I think about the beach and the distance between the foghorn and the shed and how my veggies have certainly frozen in the greenhouse in the time I've been in town. I think about the desk lined up in front of Knight Peak and the sketchpad lying on top, open to a still mostly blank page.

That night Kyle and I rent a single room at the hostel. We are tentative with each other at first. We are two different people, coming together in a space we have never before crossed.

Late that night, I lie next to Kyle watching the rain blow in the false light of the streetlamp outside the window. I am retracing the steps that got us here in my mind. "Kyle!" It surprises both of us.

He is jolted out of sleep. "What? What's wrong?"

I am sitting up in bed. "Where is the note that the halibut fisherman left? Do you have it?"

"No, why?"

"What did the handwriting look like?"

"I don't remember."

"Try. Was it small and perfect like William Harris'?"

Now Kyle is sitting up also. "Why would you think that?"

"Charles said he started building bidarkas when he was at the lighthouse, that he was selling them. You said it was a lost art, that not many people build them anymore, but the Coast Guard guy said he was having one built in Juneau. The halibut fisherman always came from the direction of Juneau. What did the handwriting look like?"

"Oh my god." Kyle is up out of bed, pulling on jeans as if he might go somewhere. "There is a guy in town who builds them, I noticed a few people paddling them around when I lived here before. That's why I decided to build one when I found that book, I'd always wanted one, ever since seeing them here. The handwriting was neat and clean."

"It's him." I say, "Why else would he show up and stare like that?"

"But how would he know we were out there?"

"It's winter in Juneau. Nobody has anything to do but gossip. They must've advertised here as well as Neely last spring. I'm sure he heard that someone moved out there. He would be interested probably since no one has chosen it since him. He would ask, hear your name—wait, why is your last name different from his?"

Kyle is pacing in the small space of the room. "I have my mom's name. She changed both of ours to her maiden name when I was three. That was when she gave up on him completely and never looked back." Kyle sits down on the edge of the bed, drops his head into his hands. "This is crazy. I hate him, I don't even want to find him anymore." He looks over. "Let's leave. Let's go to Mexico for what's left of the winter. I think I'm done with Alaska."

"How can you say that? Maybe it's not him, but maybe it is. And if it is, why not let him speak for himself? He did a lot of bad things, but maybe he's worth forgiving. Maybe he has punished himself so much by now that you could both do something different now." My voice breaks and I start to cry again as I think of William's list, his methodical carving of numbers, of Elizabeth on the ice, of that one misstep, of how I should've seen it coming. Kyle gathers me in his arms. From against his chest, I say, "Maybe you can give him one chance, see what he does with it."

21.

THE NEXT morning we're up early. Kyle has three days off before the next fishing trip he's agreed to. Over coffee, he shifts in his seat, gets up, adds more creamer to his coffee, gets up, picks up a newspaper, reads one headline and puts it back down, comes back to our table and finally says, "So what do we do? Just start asking around for him?"

I reach for his hand. "Let's start with Sarah. She knows everyone."

Down on the docks, we walk to Sarah's dad's boat. She is mending net, a big heavy black mess spread out all over the deck. "Hey," she says smiling as we walk up. "What are you guys up to? And why are you spending money at the hostel when you can stay at our house? Doug and I are fine to stay on the boat. I actually prefer it to land."

"Thanks for the offer," I say.

"Do you know of a guy named William Harris?" Kyle asks.

She shakes her head. "No. Did he fish out of here at some point? If he had, I'd probably know him."

"I don't know. He might live in town. Maybe he builds bidarkas?"

She shakes her head again. "Ted builds bidarkas. He built a couple for dad and me many years ago. He's got quite a business. There's only a couple guys in all of Southeast that still build them. He's got a shop over on Fourth Street. Who's William Harris?"

When Kyle falters, I say, "He lived at the lighthouse in the seventies."

"The guy that disappeared."

"Right," I say. I can feel Kyle deflating next to me.

Back on the street, I say, "Let's just go see anyway."

Kyle doesn't say anything, but turns with me when I turn down Fourth Street. On both sides there are big industrial buildings. We pass a propane shop and then get to one with a small sign out front that says *Juneau Bidarkas*. The building is shaped like a barn and made of corrugated metal. There are no windows, and there's a door tucked against the right hand side of the building across a crushed gravel lot.

Kyle and I stand on the wet street in front of the building, neither making a move toward it. Kyle is jittery, his face flushed. He's making me nervous. "Maybe we should come back another time," I say.

Kyle's jaw is set again, his lips in a straight line. "No. I want to see how that asshole explains himself."

"It might not be him—" I say but Kyle is already crossing the gravel, pushing the door open without knocking. I step in behind him.

The ceiling is high with a series of skylights. The workshop is warm and airy and surprisingly bright. There's a man bent over a half built bidarka balanced just above waist height by a series of custom made sawhorses. He turns when we walk in.

He is thin and weather beaten, his hair is thick and turning gray, cut trim and neat. I see it right away. The length of spine, the shape of forearms, the color of eye, the way he stands. He has not moved or taken his eyes off Kyle. They are exactly the other, twenty years apart.

"Kyle," the man says and even his voice is the same.

Kyle is across the room in under a second. He swings, catches William hard and square in the face with his fist. William goes down and stays down, blood gushing from his nose, through his hand that he has brought up to his face. Kyle stands over him for a second before he turns. A man I hadn't noticed before comes rushing over to William from the back of the shop. Kyle whips past me, out the door.

Outside, there is no wind, the fog lays heavy and thick over everything. I catch sight of Kyle already most of the way down the road and moving fast. I follow him, but do not call out or try to catch up. He walks straight ahead, not looking up. He gets to the main road, the one that runs parallel to the channel, turns and follows it south. He is moving fast enough that I need to jog to keep up. I do this for a short period of time until I realize how pointless it is to be running in full raingear after someone who does not want to be caught.

I walk back toward the hostel slowly through the steady rain, trying to figure out how you ask for forgiveness when you do not deserve it.

I fall asleep alone at the hostel that evening. Kyle comes in late. I hear him close the door quietly. Once in the room, rather than coming to bed, he sits on the edge of it. I tentatively rest one foot against him, which he reaches for. He is still sitting there when I wake in the morning.

"I'm going back," he says.

I wait for more. When nothing else comes, I ask if he wants me to come with him.

"Yes."

We walk in silence back to Fourth Street. I reach for Kyle's hand and he holds mine. He pauses a minute before he opens the door. William is bent over the same kayak on sawhorses. He turns to face Kyle. There is a small white bandage over his nose and a deep red under both eyes on its way to purple. The man who was there yesterday is struggling with a large piece of nylon spread out on a workbench. He has scissors and a measuring tape on the bench as well. He is about the same age as William, but has a slackness to his face and a clumsiness to his motions that suggests a deep rooted issue. William gestures to him, "This is Graham."

Kyle's eyes dart toward the man who looks up and smiles wide and unhindered until it seems he suddenly recognizes Kyle. "Go away," he says to Kyle who is still staring at him.

"It's okay," William says to him.

"I want him to go away," Graham says again, becoming more agitated.

"It's okay," William says again. "This is Kyle. My son," he adds tentatively. "But he's a grown man now. Can you believe it?"

"That's Kyle?" Graham asks, staring wide eyed. "It's thirty-seven days till his birthday. You said we'd never see him."

"Yeah," William says. "You're right, I didn't think we would."

When he turns back to us, he says, "Graham and I fought together. He took a bullet to the head."

Kyle's eyes dart back to Graham. "I thought—" he says and then switches track, "Look, I'm sorry about yesterday."

William shakes his head. "I deserve much worse than that."

The two men stare at each other. "I need to know why you never came home," Kyle says eventually. "And then I will leave you alone."

William's face looks old suddenly, but he doesn't drop Kyle's gaze. "I never stopped trying to."

Kyle looks away, dissatisfied.

William takes a step closer. "I was afraid. Of myself and of you and of all the ways I would fail you. And so I failed you in the worst possible way. I used to think it was to save you and I the constant disappointment it would've been otherwise, but I know now it was only that I was a coward."

Kyle considers this. "Did you steal my gun?"

"I stole my own gun from you, yes. You were going to hurt someone with it."

Kyle narrows his eyes. "It's a little late for parenting."

"I know what that lighthouse can do to a person. I wanted

you to leave before it dragged you into something you couldn't get out of. Did you know who I was or were you just shooting at someone you thought was fishing too close to your island?"

"You can't fish halibut in a thousand feet of water."

Half of a smile appears on William's face. "I thought you were fresh up from down south, that maybe you wouldn't know that."

"I've been fishing up here since I was twenty-two."

"That'd be six years," Graham chimes in.

"You've been up here that long?" William asks.

"Yes."

"How'd you even know I was out there?" Kyle asks.

"The Coast Guard posted signs around Juneau in the spring looking for someone to move out to the lighthouse. I heard someone in the bar say your name when someone else asked who was crazy enough to move out there. I couldn't believe it, I had to know if it was you or just some weird coincidence. I could tell from a distance that you were you, even though I'd never seen you before. My intention was to talk to you each time, but I couldn't do it. Every time I got there, I couldn't do it."

Kyle looks away.

William's face darkens. "I know it doesn't mean shit, but I'm sorry."

Kyle nods as he turns, this time leaving slowly, clearly having had enough.

He sleeps the rest of the morning and into the afternoon. When he wakes up, he eats the sandwich I bought him hours earlier. "Do you know what the number 29 means? Did Charles say?"

"It's the number of people he killed."

Kyle lets out a long breath. He continues to eat, both of us cross-legged on the bed in the hostel. When he finishes, we go out for a walk and end up on Fourth Street. "It's like a moth to a flame," Kyle says throwing me a sideways glance.

I can hear the saw running inside the shop. I guess by the

amount of light left in the afternoon that it is close to the end of the workday. Kyle opens the door for the third time in twenty-four hours.

William looks up. He is alone. William waits for Kyle to say something and when he doesn't, William says, "I could use some help planing these ribs down." He points to the pieces of the kayak spread between the sawhorses in front of him. I watch Kyle hesitate before he walks over, takes the hand planer from William and asks, "What's the width you need?"

William tells him and Kyle starts at one end of the wood, lines up and runs the planer evenly down the length of the wood in the way I've seen him do many times out at the lighthouse on the wood of his own kayak. I move silently to the stool where Graham had been sitting earlier in the day, not wanting to disrupt whatever is happening between them.

William finds another planer, sets up two more sawhorses and gets to work on another rib of the kayak. They work side by side for some time until Kyle asks where Graham is.

Without looking up, William says, "Hannah, his wife, picked him up. He works with me in the mornings, always has."

They continue to work, each of their bodies falling into the same long sweeping rhythm planing wood demands. After a while longer, Kyle asks, "What about that bird?"

William stops, looks up. "You know when the wind gets going out there and your skin starts crawling because there's nowhere to go?"

"Yes," Kyle says, also stopping.

"That first winter out there was really tough. I couldn't stand all the whistling and rattling. It was all I could hear. I didn't want to be one of those crazy people who talks to himself, so I just didn't talk for weeks straight until one day when this bird landed on the island. I think she was actually blown there, she couldn't fly. I fed her hot dogs. She was something else to think about, someone to talk to. She followed me around everywhere I went for most of a year before she died. I made her a bed upstairs in one of the corners on the floor and she'd hop up the stairs when it was time for bed. She never really got over the busted wing. Must've had an infection or something. I never cried so hard in my life. Sounds crazy, now."

"Oh no. I get it," Kyle says, his face moving toward a half smile for the first time, before he goes back to planing.

They work for over an hour with no other words between them. When night darkens the skylights, and Kyle finishes the rib he was working on he says, "Alright, well. See you later."

William watches us go, not moving from where he stands. "See you later," he repeats back.

The fog that has encased Juneau does not lift the next day.

"There were quite a few ribs left to plane," Kyle says over coffee. "Thought maybe I'd go back and help again this morning."

"Ok, I'll catch up to you later."

I spend the day in the woods, walk for hours concentrating on the rhythm of one foot then the other, branches woven tight overhead. The unwinding that the dizziness started has stopped. I'm as still as I have ever been.

Late in the afternoon, I walk through town to William's shop. When I step through the door, they both look up. William is wrapping thread in a tight x, securing a rib toward the back of the boat. Close by, Kyle sits with two huge sheets of nylon over his lap, slowly stitching them together.

"I thought I would stop in and introduce myself properly," I say.

William walks over and offers his hand.

"Anna Richards," I say.

His hand is rough and course against mine. "William Harris, although I haven't gone by that in years. I go by Ted now. I started over when I came to Juneau from the lighthouse." He looks from me to Kyle. "No one knows who I am here, except you two. Come to think of it, no one really knows as much about me as you two do. You never mentioned how you found me."

"You left a trail," I say. "We just followed it."

"Maybe I did." William says.

"The postcard you sent," Kyle says, "was the first clue." His eyes are flat and unsettling.

William's face drops.

"I kept it," Kyle goes on.

"I couldn't face you, Kyle," William says, the life drained out of him all at once.

"I was five." There is not anger in Kyle's voice, not yet, only truth like a brick wall. "On the back of it you wrote that you were coming home," he adds.

William runs his hand along the smooth wood of the kayak, looks down at it. "I did say that."

"I waited."

William turns then, faces Kyle. "How long are you going to do this?" I watch his hand tighten around the rib of the kayak he just added to the frame.

"What? Be pissed off? Probably forever." Kyle has not moved, I'm not sure he's even blinked.

"Then don't come back." William's words are as hard as Kyle's. "I can't take it."

"You don't abandon your family and then expect a free pass."

"I'm not looking for a free pass, Kyle. I spent your childhood doing every damn thing I could think of to make myself into someone you could look up to and guess what? I ran out of time. Did you ever consider that your life is better because I didn't come home?"

"I would've looked up to you no matter how you were."

"That was the fucking problem."

The two men stare at each other. William's face is red, Kyle is barely breathing. I am too afraid to move, afraid I will disrupt any balance that might be left.

"Look," William moves so that he is inches from Kyle's face, "I have survived two wars, one for this country and one I waged against myself, and I would do it again just to get to the day that you walked through that door and punched me in the face. I will take whatever you want to hand out but just know you might be the thing that breaks me. I have always loved you even though I never knew a thing about you."

They continue to stare at each other until Kyle looks down. He picks up the sheet of nylon spread across his lap that will slide over the skeleton of the kayak, engaging each piece of wood with all the others, everything under tension, working together to navigate the sea. "Are these stitches too far apart?" he asks William, with only a touch less aggression.

William glances down. "They need to be a little closer."

Kyle nods and goes back to work. William watches him through two more stitches and then begins to secure the next rib. They both move slowly, as if they're underwater.

I move to the workbench stool and watch them work. They fall into a measured silence. All of the questions I once had for William dissolve as I study the space each are somehow allowing for the other.

It's hard for me to attach everything I know about William to the thin man who patiently carves a three foot section of wood into a gentle curve. He works intently, or so it seems, until I notice how often his eyes slide to Kyle. Not this way, he says, that way; not my way, but this easier way, let me show you. And Kyle does.

I slip outside, back into the rain and fog to search out the municipal building. I ask a woman on the street and she points uphill, away from the harbor. I climb the hill and head toward the flagpoles. There is a sign out front and a small freshly cut lawn. I step through the heavy double doors of what seems to be the oldest building in town into a long hallway with a high, rounded ceiling.

A gentle light comes through the many windows. Phones ring behind closed doors and two people speak softly to each other at the end of the hallway.

The two closest doors are both labeled Department of Motor Vehicles. In between each door along the hallway are framed prints. The first is of Russian fur traders, some of the first white settlers in the area. The second is of a Tlinget potlatch, a traditional feast of the native tribe.

A woman moves past me, her steps loud on the wood floor. I move slowly from one picture of Alaskan life, past or present, to the next. Halfway down the hallway, I find it. The four peaks in the left hand corner, a replica of the view as seen from the desk in the room with the light; William's signature. There is nothing else to indicate he is the artist.

The sketch is a side view of a brown bear crossing a stream. Every line is full of confidence. The bear seems alive enough to breathe. She fills the page, water flows around her, the leaves of the heavy shrub at the water's edge seem to be moving in the wind. She's spotted the viewer and has stopped mid stride, one front leg lifted above the fast moving water. The shrub seems to be closing behind her where she just stepped through it.

The bear faces the viewer, the one who has seen her. In her eye is not aggression or fear, just a clear, steady look of acceptance. For how things just changed. For the way things now are. For whatever comes next.

22.

THE NEXT day, the fog lifts to the tops of the mountains and a light rain falls. Kyle goes to the docks first to tell the skipper of the *Susan Marie* that he will stay in town for this trip.

From there he heads back to William's shop and I head uphill until I am standing at the head of the trail that leads to the Mendenhall Glacier, to the Juneau Ice Field. The trail starts out like any other, under the canopy where I am safe, closed in. I keep moving, try not to think. My stomach tightens as the air cools.

The trail ends at the edge of ice. The claustrophobic feeling of the nightmare closes over me as I slowly pick my way across the wide edge of loose gravel until I am standing on the ice for the first time since the day Elizabeth died.

Without crampons, I'm forced into small tentative steps. My heart beats hard against my rib cage as I gaze up the frozen river. The top of the ice is almost the same color as the sky, a light gray that stretches as far as I can see. I think of William Harris, watching Kyle so closely, somehow living with all the choices he made, right and wrong, good and bad. I think of his list, what he left at the lighthouse.

The cool air moving down the body of the glacier rolls over me in waves. I can almost hear crampons. I close my eyes, the temperature of the ice moving through my rubber rain boots into my bones. I think of Elizabeth, how that day on the ice has become my center rib. In my mind I see her walking beside me. I see again her sure-footed, solid stride. I hold myself still, will her in my mind to keep walking on up the ice, let the distance between us grow.

*　　*　　*　　*

Late that afternoon, I stop in at the coffee shop where Sarah has picked up extra work for the winter. I stare at the wall, take small sips of my tea. Sarah walks over when there is a break in customers. Her hair flies about, half contained. She is as comfortable here as she is at home as she is on a boat. There is nothing self conscious about her.

"I made lasagna before I came into work. Doug's going to throw it in the oven around 5. Do you guys want to come over?"

"That'd be great."

"Everything okay?" She sits down in the chair across from me.

I glance up at her kind face. It seems there is not much left of my resolve to keep anything buried. "Seems like what comes next for me isn't what comes next for Kyle."

She takes a deep breath, lets it out audibly. "We're in the same situation," she says. "Do you mean you want to stay at the lighthouse and he doesn't?"

"Yeah."

"How much longer is your lease?"

"Another three months. I don't know if I'm brave enough to be out there alone for that long. How are you in the same situation?"

An uncomfortable look crosses her face. "Doug and I have been saving for a boat for as long as we've been together. It's been our dream, to fish together on our own. But since we lost Andrew, I don't think that's what he wants to do anymore, but it's still exactly what I want to do."

"What else would Doug do?"

She shrugs. "Work in town. Probably at the shipyard."

"You can hire deckhands. Seems like you'd make a good captain, even without Doug. I'm sure he will be real happy to see you when you get back to town."

She smiles. "And I'll bet Kyle will be happy to see you when you get back."

Over the next few days, the temperature continues to drop. On the trails, the leafless branches of the blueberry are slowly encased in smooth ice and the moss becomes hard underfoot.

Each morning, Kyle and I have coffee together, then he walks to the shop. It is understood that he will finish the kayak with William. We don't talk about what's next after that. We are still on uneven ground, afraid of slipping. Each night, we sleep as close as possible.

One morning, I walk the streets down to the water. I sit on a bench and watch the wind and rain move across the shore and down the channel. Slowly, it turns to snow, begins to pile in the creases of my raingear. Underneath, I'm warm in several layers of wool. The low clouds pack the valleys as the channel turns white.

"Anna?"

I turn to see Doug, buried in his raingear as well. "Hey."

"What are you doing?" he asks.

"Watching the storm."

"While you sit out in it?" He sits down next to me.

"How's work?" I ask. He has picked up winter work fiber-glassing a boat.

"Fine, just taking a break. I was going to get coffee." He relaxes against the bench and settles his gaze down the channel. "Snow's a nice change, huh?" he says.

"Yeah."

A slow silence fills the space between us. "You know," he says after awhile, "I was telling Sarah last night, the only thing I remember clearly from that night is your voice. I had no idea where I was or what had happened, but I kept hearing your voice somewhere in the background and it made me feel like things would somehow right themselves."

I keep my eyes on the channel.

"I still can't believe you came out after me," he adds.

"I had to."

He looks over. "Why?" And then it happens again. The past unveiled. All that work to hide it, over. I tell him of ice like concrete, that morning, that night. There are no locks left, only water rushing.

As the momentum of the words slows and then stops, I meet Doug's eyes. I find no judgment, only level ground, a place where I can say all these things and remain standing.

"I've always thought it was my fault," I add.

"Sounds like she knew her own mind. I wonder if you really could've changed it."

"It's that I encouraged it."

He looks at me. "Isn't that what we're supposed to do for people we care about?"

The next day, I go with Kyle to the shop. William and Graham are already at work when we walk in. They've got the skin of the boat stretched over the skeleton. It is sewn at the bow and the stern and hangs open across the top. William glances up when we walk in. "Your stitches look good."

Kyle's face does not change, but I see that he is pleased.

"How are you, Anna?" William asks.

"Fine. Hi Graham," I add.

"Hi." He turns to Kyle, "Twenty-nine days to your birthday."

"That's right," Kyle says. He runs a hand along the smooth wood of the kayak.

William says to him, "Next, you'll need to stitch up the middle. Start here where the cockpit will go, pull toward the bow before each stitch, so there's no sagging." He demonstrates and Kyle watches. William's hands are smooth and fast as he goes through the practiced motions of his craft. The curved needle slides through the two layers of nylon skin and it pulls together tightly around the boat.

"How much slack do I leave?" Kyle asks.

William shakes his head. "It's all feel. You'll get it. Just pull it snug. Follow the line of that first stitch."

Kyle pulls a stool up to the side of the kayak and begins the work of imitating over and over what William did first.

I sit down on the stool over by the workbench, out of the way.

William looks over. "I could use some help with the cockpit," he says to me.

He pulls wood from a long thin trough where it has been soaking in hot water. He shows me how to bend it, work it into the correct shape, and then how to keep it there. Later he shows me where to drill the holes, so that Kyle can eventually sew it into place. We work in the diffused light that filters in from the cold day. Graham keeps the stove full of wood scraps so that it stays warm inside the shop.

Kyle stays bent to his task, one stitch after another, the skin pulling tighter and tighter, showing off the long smooth curves of the boat. When William walks over to check his progress, Kyle says, "This would've been a hard step to learn from that book."

William nods. "You've been teaching yourself from the book at the lighthouse?"

"Yeah. A good winter project."

"Most folks that try to build from books end up with a kayak that doesn't float. You should've seen the first one I built. Yours looked pretty tight. I couldn't believe it when I walked into the shed and saw it."

I measure carefully, mark the spot where I will drill the next hole in the cockpit, remembering the shards of sharp wood, half the ribs hanging from the frame, split in two, the rest of Kyle's kayak on the floor in splinters.

Later that afternoon, William and I are sitting next to the stove on folding chairs. He is checking my work, looking for any irregularities in the wood, anywhere it might split due to the bending that would mean we had to start over. "Did it help you?" I ask him. "Being out at the lighthouse?"

He looks up, rests the round oval of wood on his lap. "I left there changed. Guess that's what I was looking for." He goes back to inspecting the wood and then stops, sets it in his lap again. "Did you two find my—list of names?"

"Yes," I say and see the impact of it on his body.

"Did Kyle see it?" he asks slowly.

"He knows you killed that many men."

William nods slowly and picks up the cockpit. As his hands begin moving again, I see that they are shaking slightly.

Kyle continues to stitch through the afternoon after Graham goes home. I split wood and keep the woodstove burning. William gives me small tasks, but mostly I watch the two men work side by side. When Kyle takes a break, I inspect his work along with William. Each stitch is evenly spaced, none any bigger or smaller than the first one done by William.

"What's left after he finishes the stitching?" I ask.

"Not much," William says. "I'll trim the excess skin, then he'll go over it with a quick stitch to tuck it in, then we'll place the cockpit and that gets sewn in and then she's ready."

Kyle glances up, then both men look away. Kyle's speed slows and William does not begin trimming the excess. We stand around, watch Kyle stitch.

"Maybe you guys could build a kayak for Kyle next," I say, not really looking at either of them.

Kyle stops what he is doing.

"I need to tell you—"

Kyle's face tightens at my tone.

"I destroyed it."

Kyle stares at me.

"With a hammer."

His face falls.

"I was mad," I explain.

"A hammer?" he says.

"When the cutter went by and tapped the horn twice and you

weren't on it, I was so mad, I just, I don't know."

"How much of it…" Kyle asks. "Did you hit with the hammer?"

"Well…most of it," I say feeling terrible.

"One thing's for sure," William says to Kyle, a slow smile spreading across his face. "As long as you stick with her, life's never going to get boring."

Kyle shakes his head while holding William's eyes, a fraction of the humor in William's face sneaking into his own.

William rubs the calluses of one hand over the calluses of the other, still smiling. "We could start one for you after this one. If you want." And then he adds, less confidently, "I'd like that."

That night I tell Kyle I want to go back out to the lighthouse alone. We are next to each other in the soft bed of our single room at the hostel. We can hear people in the hall outside our door, but inside the room it's cozy and dark. He runs his hand down my arm. "I'll go back out there with you," he says.

"You're miserable out there. Besides, it's something I need to do on my own."

"And then what?" he asks.

"Then I want to come back here, to you. Maybe we go to Mexico, maybe we live in Juneau for awhile. What do you think?"

"I think I need to keep taking this one day at a time," he says, rolling onto his side, pulling me closer. "You really want to go out there by yourself?"

I stare at the textured wall next to the bed, Kyle's body tight against the back of mine, his arm around me, our hands intertwined. "I need to finish what I started," I say softly.

"Okay," he whispers, his mouth close to my ear. "Then, I'll meet you right here on the last day of the lease."

"Sorry I busted up your kayak."

"That's okay. It might not have floated, anyway."

We listen to loud voices coming from the kitchen of the

hostel and then laughter.

"Maybe I'll go to Mexico for three months," Kyle says, his mouth still next to my ear.

"You wouldn't let me shiver my ass off out at the lighthouse while you lay on the beach."

"I might." There is a smile in Kyle's voice.

I roll over so I can see his face. "You don't want to stay? Spend a little more time with William?"

A pained look crosses his face. "I don't know. It would be so easy to just get on the ferry tomorrow and be done with it. Half the time I hate him and the other half I can't believe I'm in the same room with him. The thing that gets me is what you said, that he's not all bad. It'd be easier if he was."

On the day Kyle and William start cutting the cedar into long thin strips that will become a bidarka for Kyle, I walk over to the Coast Guard office.

I wait for Lieutenant Lawrence at the front desk. Again, he comes down the hall and shakes my hand. "Good to see you, Anna. Come on back."

We sit down in his office chatting for a minute about the snow, about the kids ice skating on the slough at the edge of town now that it was frozen over.

Eventually I say, "I've decided to go back out to the light-house on my own. Kyle's going to stay in town."

The Lieutenant stares at me. Blinks. Doesn't say anything. I see that he is measuring me against the channel, against what the weather will likely do in the next three months.

"Are you sure?" he finally says. "It's the government—all you have to do is sign another document to unsign the first one."

"I'm sure."

He nods. "Okay," he says slowly. "In that case, I'll have the cutter stop on their patrols to check in, see that everything's alright. And you can catch a ride with them any time you want to come back to Juneau. And if you change your mind, don't hesitate—"

"I'll be fine. I'll be ready to come back to town when the lease is up in March."

"The next patrol leaves in two weeks, if you want to catch a ride out then."

"Doug and Sarah offered to run me out there at the next break in the weather."

"Alright." He turns around, opens a drawer behind his desk and digs around. "Then take this." He hands over a satellite phone.

"I don't need—"

"I know you don't need it, but if you're going to be out there alone, I want you to be able to get a hold of me if you need to." He looks at me across the desk. "Nobody wants to broadcast their troubles on Channel 16 with the whole fleet listening in. If you need anything at all, call me directly."

23.

IT TAKES almost a week for the weather to calm down enough for us to make the trip to the lighthouse. Kyle walks us down to the dock, holds me close, while Doug and Sarah rearrange all the boxes of my supplies on the boat, working to even out the weight for the trip. I breathe in the skin of Kyle's smooth neck. "I should come with you," he offers one last time.

"You need to keep figuring out your relationship to your Dad."

He nods distractedly.

"And I need to keep hashing through my relationship with myself," I add.

"Don't take the skiff out, okay?"

"I won't. Unless it's really calm out."

He gives me an exasperated look. "The oil for the light is in the corner of the shed where the scaffolding was. If you oil once every ten days, you should have enough to last the three months."

"Okay."

Sarah and Doug have finished rearranging boxes and are now shuffling around, trying to look busy while we finish our goodbye. Kyle pulls me close again and says into my ear, "Thanks for understanding that I need to stay."

I nod into his shoulder, breathe deep his smell one last time and then climb over the caprail to keep from crying in front of everyone.

There's a thin layer of ice on the skiff and the sky is a pale blue as we pull out of the harbor. Kyle stands with his hands in his pockets watching us navigate between boats and then out into the channel. As he falls away behind us, I swallow hard against the tears, pull my hat down firmly over my ears and wiggle my toes in my boots to keep them warm. As the harbor falls away behind us, I walk into the small covered wheelhouse.

"You okay?" Sarah asks.

I nod, not trusting my voice. In my mind I see Kyle as he must be, still standing on the dock, watching us. I want to tell Doug to turn around and I want to keep moving north toward the light-house in equal measure. It is not that I want to be without Kyle, it's that I need to be with myself before I can be with Kyle. Doug rests his hand loosely on the steering wheel and Sarah sits in the co-captain's chair. I settle onto the cushioned bench behind them.

As the skiff reaches full speed, the rocking settles into a gentle pounding over the tops of the waves. The sound of the dual out-boards fills up the wheelhouse so there is no need for any of us to talk. Instead, we all watch the steep forested walls of the channel pass. There are a group of eagles on the shore eating something at one point and a pod of killer whales that Doug slows down for. Eventually the lighthouse appears on the horizon. As it rises out of the sea before us, I feel something in my chest rise to meet it.

"Your skiff's still floating. That's good." Doug says as it comes into view around the corner of the island.

As we bump up against the beach, I climb over. We pass box-es between us, moving the supplies off the boat onto the beach. When we're done, Doug says, "Sarah and I will put the boat on the haulout and row in. We'll be up in a bit."

"Okay." I pick up the closest box and head up the path to the house.

As I walk up the gentle swell of the island, the mountains rise above me, and the water moves in a graceful arc around the land. The same feeling I had the first time I stood here fills me again. A small seed of peace, growing.

I walk through the front door into the kitchen, set my box down. I sit in the rocking chair for a bit, take in the room.

Everything is familiar and welcoming. All the energy I poured into this space to make it livable is now offered back to me.

I walk up the stairs, through the trapdoor. The sea is calm, the wind is just starting to move on its surface.

I start where I always start, trace valleys and peaks with my eyes.

Doug and Sarah come into view, standing on the beach on the west side of the island. They are looking across the water to where the boat sank. I watch them lean in to each other, her hand reaching for his.

They are on their way back toward the house, still hand in hand, as I step out the front door. When they get closer, Sarah says, "Will you give us a tour? I've never actually been on the island."

We carry the boxes that Doug and Sarah have carried up to the front door inside and then start the tour with the kitchen. Doug admires the hand built cupboards and Sarah peers inside the cookstove. "You actually cook on this thing?"

"It only took about thirty loaves to figure out how to make bread in it. Works out the best if you bake it in that warming drawer, if that's what it is."

"That's awesome." Her eyes are animated. She checks out the hose I ran from the cistern into the kitchen and notices the lack of mildew and mold in the room. I feel proud when she notices the way wood is stacked neatly next to the cookstove and the woodstove. "It's so ordered and neat in here, feels like an actual house. I thought it would have an institutional feel, like the Coast Guard office, or something."

"That's how it felt at first."

"Can we see the light?" Doug asks.

We walk up the stairs and the ladder until we are all standing on the platform around the light.

"Wow," Sarah says, turning in a circle, looking from one window to the next.

"Everything looks different from this height, doesn't it?" Doug says as he walks over to the closest window and gazes toward Juneau. "More friendly, almost."

Doug wanders over to the light and asks a few questions about how it works. While we talk, Sarah examines the spotlight, rests a hand on each handle, pulls it back as far as it can go as Kyle would've done that night Doug and I were on the beach. She stands there for a moment and then walks back over to the windows.

"Hey Doug," she says, turning around. "The winds picking up. We probably ought to get going."

He glances up, agrees.

On the way down the stairs, Sarah says, "I've never noticed the greenhouse, all the times I've passed by here on the boat."

"We built it. We had tomatoes all the way into November."

"Did you heat it?"

"With charcoal."

"Brilliant! I've heard of people building them next to the house to help keep it warm. Charcoal in a wood stove?"

"A leaky wood stove."

She laughs. "Whatever works, right?"

I walk with them down to the beach. Before they climb into the skiff, Sarah turns to me and says, "Since Doug's decided not to fish, Dad and I need a deckhand in the spring." Behind her, I catch the slight nod of Doug's head. The look on her face is both sad and determined.

"I don't know anything about fishing," I tell her.

"You'll learn. Besides, you're the only one Dad and I agree on."

"They're not so bad to work for," Doug says, as I try to imagine myself commercial fishing. I imagine being out on the water I've come to know in my time at the lighthouse but only for four or five days at once, with time in town in between. A more balanced existence. I imagine Kyle fishing on another boat, or working in William's shop, finding an apartment together, buying a couch.

"So you'll do it?" Sarah asks.

"Yeah. I'll give it a try."

"Great!" She gives me a hug good-bye as Doug drags the inflatable dingy down to the water and they both climb in. As he grabs the oars to row them back out to the skiff, he says, "See you in the spring, Anna."

"See you then," I say.

That afternoon, I build a big fire in the woodstove to chase out the damp cold as the rain beats up the channel. I unpack all the food, set some dough to rising and make tea. I eat a bean and rice burrito for dinner early and spend the rest of the daylight hours in front of the fire, holding still, letting everything catch up to me.

That night, when I climb into bed, the light swinging around the room, I notice drops of dried blood on my pillow. My mind flashes to the drops of blood forever frozen into the ice shelf. I sit and stare. It occurs to me that life moves in patterns, unless you break them. William would've gone on hiding except that Kyle stood in front of him and demanded that he show himself, which he did. I will go on falling until I catch myself.

That night, the nightmares return. Elizabeth and I are walking along together on the surface of the ice. I see her slip at the edge of the crevasse. I watch her try to right herself, keep from going in and then I watch her fall. I try to jump in after her, but the ice closes. There is no evidence of a crevasse, only ice so smooth I can see my reflection in it. I wake up cold, screaming Elizabeth's name. The light has turned off, the day has begun.

I lie there for a minute, shivering under the covers, wondering what I've done, if isolating myself so much will indeed vault me back toward people or start the slow unwinding toward permanent instability.

I get out of bed, build up the fire in the cookstove, make a strong pot of coffee, knead the dough and set it into loaves. I spread out the fire, get it just right for the bread. In the shed I find the oil can and bag of tools for performing the light maintenance. I carry everything upstairs and try to remember what I'd seen Kyle do. By the time I'm done my stomach is growling. It's closer to lunch then dinner and the bread is ready. I spread jam and make myself a salad with all the fresh veggies I bought in town.

After lunch, I inspect the damage in the greenhouse. There is one pepper plant that might make it. All the dead plants get tossed in the ocean, all the five gallon buckets full of soil get moved to the middle. I close up everything, wondering if it will ever be used again, and carry the pepper plant into the house. The tall spindly plant is long past producing any more peppers, but it will be nice to have something else alive in the house with me.

The rest of the first day passes getting caught up on the chores of the house, as does most of the first week. Each morning there is a break in the rain, so I continue with the painting. Kyle and I had finished two sides of the house and had just moved the scaffolding to the third side, which I finish painting that week. I tie myself in with a length of rope I find in the shed that doesn't look too old. I keep the sat phone on my person, so I can call for help if I find myself dangling or in a heap on the ground.

Every night the nightmare repeats itself, except that somewhere in the second week of my time alone at the lighthouse, Elizabeth becomes something terrible. She is frozen into the walls of the glacier, her hair wet and stringy, her lips blue, blood all over her face, her eyes open, watching me. I wake kicking at the covers, launching out of bed, trying to get away. The dream doesn't stop until I am standing in the room, several feet from the bed, breathing hard.

I run up the ladder to the room with the light. It is still dark out, the light swings behind me as I fold into a corner and pull my knees up to my chest. It is warm, the last heat of the woodstove has gathered at this highest point. I lean my head against the glass, hands shaking, and wait for daylight.

Hours later, when the day begins to brighten the high, gray cloud cover, I uncurl my body from the corner and sit down in front of Knight Peak. I cannot stomach food or coffee. I feel hollowed out, stripped of everything. Knight Peak is a little hazy with so much rain between me and it, but I can make out the steep north face and the slow curl of glacier along its side. I take William's list out of the drawer and set it on the desk face down.

On the back of his list I draw the first line and the next and the next, trying not to think, trying to accept this for what it is, a mountain, a river of ice, a sorrow, a heavy guilt, a horrible history, a part of me, but not all of me.

For the next two weeks, I spend every morning in the room with the light. I draw every detail. Each day defines itself as I finish the top of Knight Peak, the smooth arc of the top of the glacier, its uneven face. I sketch the surrounding mountains, the valleys as they run into the sea, the trees as they hold the landscape together, the rain as it alternately hides and shows everything.

The effort of not turning away from it exhausts me. Some afternoons, I fall asleep in the chair next to the stove while I wait for bread to rise or the rain to stop long enough for me to get more painting done on the house. With every new section of glacier I transfer to paper, less of it is with me at night.

The clouds roll in, thick and heavy, on the afternoon that I finish. I sit in the fading light of the day and look at what I have drawn, what I have added to William's list. What I will leave here when I go.

I think about William and Kyle working together in town, tying one frail piece of the kayak to the next. I think about the three of us surrounded by so much water on this cold gray coast, everything to navigate from here. I think about how what happened will never be okay, but that doesn't mean each of us can't flex in the waves, can't move with the wind instead of against it.

I fold the paper along its creases and place it back in the drawer. Take the phone number out of my pocket. The last two numbers have faded, will not be legible with time. I think back to the day I searched out the number. How I found it listed in an old newspaper article online announcing a funeral that I had not been invited to. How I had picked up the phone, dialed the number that day and found that I could not speak.

The sat phone is next to the marine radio on the desk. I press ON, wait for it to connect to the satellites. I have not used one since that morning on the ice when I called Brad to tell him Elizabeth was missing. I glance up at Knight Peak, there is only an outline of it left in the last bit of day.

I punch in each number, hesitate over the last one. I close my eyes, and press the last number. I listen to the first ring, each muscle of my body locking into place. On the second ring, the light behind me clicks on. I have not hung up yet. The third ring begins.

"'lo?" His voice is quick, business-like even though I have dialed his home number.

"May I speak with Mrs. Lowenstein?" My voice sounds pressure-cooked. I try to control my breathing.

"May I ask who's calling?"

I consider lying.

"Anna." He is not expecting me. A lot of people are named Anna. He sets the phone down. I hear him call his wife.

There is the sound of heels on a hard floor and then she picks up. "Yes?"

"This is Anna Richards."

There is a heavy silence.

"Anna?" She finally says, her voice broken open over my name.

"Yes." I close my eyes. "Please don't hang up. I want to tell you what I know of Elizabeth. And I want to tell you that I'm sorry. I was responsible for her and I didn't keep what happened from happening." The light swings behind me, lights up Knight Peak so that I see the darkening shape of it against the sky.

"She went to your tent that night. You weren't there," she says. My own brick wall of truth there is no getting around.

I focus on breathing. "Right. I should've been there. I should've seen it coming."

I fight against the way my voice shakes and go on to tell her how much Elizabeth affected me, how she mattered to me, how I am still learning what she meant when she said let it all out, how I needed to scream and spin until I fell on the ice and how she somehow saw it before I did. How she forgave so quickly and how I wanted to, was working to.

Elizabeth's mom begins to cry softly.

While the night continues to darken around me and the light makes it's slow revolutions behind me, I tell her how kind she was to Stephanie, how strong and confident she was out on the ice, how she set the pace that the other kids worked to maintain. I say it all, not stopping until I'm done. When I finish talking, there is another long silence, into which I add, "I don't mean to drag you back into the past, it's just that I've needed to say this to you but have been too afraid."

"That doesn't sound like the Elizabeth I knew," she says through her tears. I hold still, tears running down my cheek as well. "I wish I could've seen her out there, like that," she says just above a whisper, and then "Thank you. Thank you for this." And then the line is clear.

I keep the phone to my ear, listen to the empty silence. Eventually I set the phone down, raise my eyes to the night. Far below me, I see the running lights of a boat moving through the water, back toward Juneau. The light flashes behind me, illuminating the edges of the island, each dangerous rock, and the far shore. I stand and watch the boat adjust its course according to what the light has shown him.

Acknowledgments

There are many people who have guided and supported me along the way as a writer. When I first began to write fiction, I was living in a small cabin on the beach in Alaska without power. While we had a generator, it was loud and drank gas about as fast as you could fill it. Tara Alcock and the rest of the Petersburg Public Library staff took pity on me spread out on the floor next to a plug in the hallway hours before the library opened and generously let me use a room not usually available to library patrons where I'm sure I typed at least 200,000 words.

Max Regan, a brilliant teacher and editor, has offered me nothing but steady encouragement since I sat nervously in the first writing class I'd ever taken, fourteen years ago. Anytime I get stuck in my writing, he can get me unstuck.

I am eternally grateful to Claudia Savage, one of my most trusted readers, who is always able to see the clearing while I'm still in the trees.

Thanks to Robert and Elizabeth at Ig for all their hard work. Special thanks to my agent Susan Ramer who has been a steadfast advocate for me. Her valuable input on the last few drafts of this book turned me into a much better writer.

This book would still be half done if it weren't for the efforts of my husband, Mike Demmings, who never wavered in his ability and willingness to care for our twins single-handedly in the first year of their lives to create the windows of time I needed to finish the book.